FINAL RUIN

C.G. HARRIS

Hot Chocolate Press

The Judas Files *a 5-book action-packed, supernatural series filled with snarky characters & dark humor.*

The Judas Files Completed Series:

Book 1-THE NINE

Book 2-NEW DOMINION

Book 3-ARTFUL EVIL

Book 4 - WAR ORIGIN

Book 5 - FINAL RUIN

<u>Download the **FREE SHORT STORY,**</u> Exiled

Join the C.G. Harris Legion
Join the C.G. Harris Legion to receive book intel, useless trivia, special giveaways, plus you'll learn about Hula Harry and get his Drink of the Week.
https://www.cgharris.net/legion-sign-up-page

Printed in the United States of America: First Printing, 2022
Hot Chocolate Press, Fort Collins, Colorado
Cover design by: Karri Klawiter

WWW.CGHARRIS.NET

CHAPTER ONE

True pain is never limited to simple physical agony. Suspended in a weightless void of torment with no hope of reprieve, I writhed as the flesh seared from my body, bones bent, twisted and crushed. Every breath filled my lungs with noxious razorblades. The very tissue that made me whole, torn away in ragged chunks all in an impossible never-ending cycle. My body was never spent, the agony never ended. No matter how I thrashed or screamed I could never pull away.

My eyes suffered the most brutal agony of all. All around me, amongst the raging heat and searing flames, I watched as every sorrow and regret from my life was reenacted in agonizing detail. Anger, sadness and despair consumed me with each horrible memory. Events so horrible and muddled by time that they were indistinguishable from reality. The mind is torture's greatest playground. Mine had been broken for centuries.

A glimmer of the impossible caught my eye. At first I thought it was a new torment to brutalize my mind. A promise of hope where instead disparity saturated every breath. I resolved to ignore it, but the draw was too powerful. The possibility of escape too tempting. I flailed against my weightless prison and found I could move. Only inches at a time, but it was possible. Like swimming through boiling oil, every action was an exercise in agony, but I had grown accustomed to this physical torture.

The glimmer grew to a sparkle and the sparkle to a light. I swam through the murky horrors, ignoring the pain and images that lured me back into their ritual comfort and depravity. The light got brighter as I pushed through and fought the agony.

I broke the surface of my sulfureous prison with a sputtering breath like the ugly birth of a monster. I struggled to the edge, wiping at my eyes, coughing and spitting. The churning surface thrashed and roiled, threatening to pull me under again but I managed to make it over to the side and hoist myself onto the rough crusty dirt.

My vision remained blurred while every nerve ending screamed with pain. But I was free. I wanted to cry and laugh and shout with joy, then I felt a hand on my chest. A warden perhaps, here to thrust me back into my torturous prison. I would not go.

The image of my assailant was murky but I could see well enough to defend myself. I swung a fist out in a wild arc then rolled to the side, taking care not to fall back into the sulfur pool. I tried to get to my feet, but my attacker was too fast. My legs were wrapped up in a tangle of arms before I could get them under me to run.

"Gabe, calm down." A woman's voice. "It's me. You're safe. I've got you."

Gabe? The name meant nothing to me. That wasn't my name … was it? The thought made me pause as I realized I had no idea.

"Who are you?" I wiped at my eyes trying to clear out the muck and saw a beautiful woman with long blue hair and milky white skin covered in tattoos. She reminded me of a circus runway model gone terribly right.

"Take it easy." She crawled up and sat on my legs, never

losing contact with me as if she feared I might get up and run if I had the chance. She was right.

"We've been waiting for you for weeks. I know this is a little overwhelming, but you have to trust me. I'm a friend and I'm here to help."

I watched her, trying to decide if I should believe her or not. I looked around and saw the pool I had just crawled out of. The edge was a crusted yellow leading into a boiling lime green liquid which reeked of rotten eggs. Beneath the surface I could see the impossible glowing flames that burned down below and wondered how many others were trapped inside that torturous prison. As my eyes went up I saw a field of never-ending pools similar to mine. Some larger, some smaller, but all roiling with the same glowing, sulfureous torment.

"These are the Gnashing Fields," The woman said. "And it is no small miracle that we found you. I forgot how big this place is. If it weren't for Quack I don't know if we would have."

The panic of unsurety and confusion rose inside me again and I had a sudden urge to run. Whoever this person was, she knew me, and I had no idea if that was good or bad.

She must have seen the growing unease in my face because she slowed her speech and movements to more of a calming demeanor.

"Take it easy. Like I said, we're friends. I'm Alex. We're partners."

"Partners? What kind of partners? Life partners? I don't even know you lady." I began to flail my legs to get away again, but Alex held on tight.

"Okay, partners may have been the wrong word to use. Don't worry about that right now. We are friends. We're here to help. Your memory is gone but it will come back over time. Your name is Gabriel Gantry, but everyone calls you Gabe."

Her words calmed me a bit and hearing my memories would come back felt somewhat comforting even though I had no idea why I had lost them in the first place or what the new ones might bring.

"Please don't call me that."

Alex screwed up her face in confusion. "Call you what?"

"Gabe. It sounds so … I don't know, provincial. If my name is Gabriel then call me that."

Alex rolled her eyes. "Okay, this going to be interesting. Gabriel it is … for now. Look, there is a lot to take in and I need you to try and stay calm. We have been here for a long time, well not the Gnashing Fields but— "

"Where is here? Where am I?" I looked down and realized for the first time since my muck covered rebirth that I was not wearing any clothes.

I let out a screech and did my best to cover my embarrassing bits with my hands. The sulfureous oily liquid that had clung to my body seemed to be melting away leaving me feeling dry, cold and exposed. "Woah, could you turn your head or something."

Alex raised an eyebrow. "Promise you won't run?" She developed a mischievous grin that I could not help but find a little attractive.

"Yes, I promise, just look up at the sky or something."

Alex snorted out a laugh and complied. Then she rolled off me and slung off a large backpack.

"We brought you some clothes." She reached in without looking down and tossed me a pair of jeans and a t-shirt.

I took them and pulled on the pants as fast as I could, then struggled into the shirt and got to my feet, still barefoot on the rough crusty ground. Alex stood up as well, looking ready to take me down with a rugby tackle if I even thought about making a run for it.

"You keep saying we." I finished straightening my shirt and fastened the button fly Levi's that fit tight enough to classify as latex paint. Who would wear a pair of self-inflicted thigh tourniquets like this? I didn't say anything though. I was just happy to have something to cover my naked body. "Is someone here with you? And you still haven't told me where we are."

"I'm not sure how to break this to you so I am just going to say it. Try to stay calm and know that I have a lot more to explain." Alex looked more than a little ready to pounce. It was cute but I was a full-grown man. If I really wanted to get away, I doubted there was much she could do to overpower me.

"Fine. Hit me. Was I kidnapped and taken to the deserts of Africa? Where are we?"

Alex opened her mouth to speak but instead I heard a voice that would never come out of someone as lovely as her.

"It's about time." This voice sounded like an east coast gangster who had smoked way too many cigars. "Did you break the big news? Sorry about the whole dead thing but Hell's not so bad once you get used to it. At least you're supposed to be here. I'm still alive but here I am, circling the Gnashing Fields looking for you. My wings have had it. I'm molting like a wet piñata. Can we get out of here?"

I stared down at the source of the grating chatter and could not believe my ears … head … wherever the voice was coming from. A coal black duck waddled up from around the far side of a roiling pool as if it should be the most natural thing for anyone to see in a field of boiling sulfur. I may not have my memory but I knew ducks should never, ever, be able to talk to humans.

Maybe now was a good time to run after all.

CHAPTER TWO

"Did he just say dead?" I pointed at the waddling menace and took a step back.

"Way to ease him into this whole thing." Alex glared at the duck, and I swear the creature responded by way of a shrug.

"How was I supposed to know you hadn't told him yet. You were here for like an hour."

"We were here for five minutes."

"Plenty of time in my estimation."

Neither of them noticed me creeping away in horror. I was a good six steps away when Alex turned to find me no longer within easy reach.

"Are you talking to that thing, too? How is that possible? I can't be dead. I was just alive." The thought gave me pause. Actually, I couldn't remember being alive … or dead. I was breathing, thinking and panicking. Dead people didn't do any of those things, did they?

"I have to get out of here." Before Alex or her feathered companion could react, I turned and sprinted away. I heard Alex shout, but I couldn't quite hear what she said. I didn't care. I wanted out of that place. Out of this nightmare I had woken into.

As luck would have it, I ran the right way. I must have burbled up on the outskirts of the Gnashing Fields because I cleared them within a few seconds. God only knew how big a place like that could be, and I made it my personal goal to never find out.

My situation did not improve away from the festering pools, though. I wanted to keep running, but the shock of my surroundings weighed me down like a boat anchor. I slowed and surveyed the scene. Red skies, barren ground and a whole city made of scrap metal and twisted iron. It resembled Satan's junkyard more than a town. Were it not for the tall catwalks and meandering people I might have thought it was just that. The smell of sulfur clung to the air and somehow I felt as though I was missing something. Everyone was bundled up. Wrapped from head to toe in old coats, blankets, and rags. They acted as if they were freezing, but I stood there in my compression jeans and t-shirt feeling toasty as a day-old bagel.

"Like I said, I have a lot to tell you."

A squeak escaped my lips and I jumped. I turned to see Alex, pedaling up behind me on a rusty oversized tricycle.

"You can't just run off. There are dangerous things out here and it'll be night soon. You do not want to be out here at night."

I spun in a full circle, taking in my impossible surroundings.

"How can this possibly get any worse?"

"Trust me. You'll settle into all of this. For now, let's go for a drink and I'll fill you in on the essentials."

I nodded. "Okay. Where are you parked?"

Alex raised an eyebrow. "I'm parked right here. Lesson one. Cars are a rarity around here. We like to go green."

I glanced at the crumbling mess of rusted circus metal. "I am not riding that."

Alex snorted out a laugh. "Don't worry. I just borrowed this from a friend. It's no Maserati, but when you need a ride, a Yugo will do in a pinch."

"That is not a Yugo. It's an anal debasement for a grizzly bear."

Alex covered her face with her hands. "This is going to be a long couple of weeks."

I opened my mouth to respond but was distracted by the sound of flapping wings and a sudden thud on the ground behind me. I turned to see the coal-dust duck righting itself from a less than graceful landing.

It looked up. "I am sick of circling in a holding pattern while you two chit-chat. Use those curled-up skin hooks for something useful and *gently* put me in that backpack." The duck stretched out a wing and motioned to the bag Alex wore on her back. "Then step off your ivory tower and ride piggyback on this three-wheeled excuse for transportation."

I stared at the duck. When I didn't move, he flared his wings, dipped his head and charged me like a feathered cobra chicken, quacking like a maniac.

"I said put me in the pack and get on that trike." He shrieked into my mind.

I yipped and ran around to the other side of Alex like a child hiding behind his mommy.

"Tell me the truth," I said. "Am I going to hear the thoughts of every animal now that I am … you know."

"Dead? No. He's the only one. You and I are just lucky that way." Alex smiled, as if she enjoyed this a little more than she should. "If I were you, I'd do what he says, though."

I peered down at the fluffed-up waterfowl and tilted my head. "Do you have a name? Is there something I should call you?"

"Don't get me started." The duck bristled and smoothed its feathers to look a little less threatening. "You can call me Quack."

I laughed then caught myself when he glared at me with his beady black eyes.

"Something funny about that name?"

"No," I said, barely able to restrain a chuckle. "It just seems a little spot on. Doesn't it get a little confusing when you're … quacking?"

I picked up Quack, then set him into the open backpack, keeping him at arm's length the whole time. "It's sort of like me running around screaming Gabriel, Gabriel, Gabriel."

Quack bit me on the finger.

"Ouch." I jumped back, shaking my hand.

"I'm sorry my name does not please you," Quack said. "Lodge a complaint with the moronic meatbag who gave me that name as soon as you see him again."

I shifted my gaze to Alex and held out my finger. Call me a toddler. "He bit me! Is he always like this?"

Alex nodded and pushed away my hand in a playacting gesture. "Sometimes he's grouchy. Step onto my bear defiler and I'll pedal us to a nice friendly place where we can talk about it."

She nodded to the low-slung basket hung between the back wheels. "Step on and off we go."

She straightened, putting her hands on the handlebars, waiting for me to comply. I looked around for a moment and took a breath. I had no idea who I was or what I was doing here. I needed a way to figure things out. If this woman was willing to help, maybe I should listen.

I stepped into the basket, put my hands on her shoulders, then Alex pushed off and started pedaling.

Besides, how much weirder could things get?

CHAPTER THREE

My piggyback tricycle ride raised more questions than it answered. I took in the sights and sounds as we squeaked through the nightmarish landscape, but my prospects didn't seem to improve. We wove deeper and deeper into a jumbled labyrinth of corrugated steel shanties, steel catwalks and a near suffocating sense of depression. Hordes of people meandered the pathways and makeshift streets where the acrid stench of burning oil drums belched tarry smoke into the air.

My memories were a little more than a greasy smear in the back of my brain, but I knew no place should be like this. The farther we rode, the more my mind rejected the reality of what my eyes saw. This had to be some sort of mistake; a place in a third world country where prosperity and hope had long ago drowned in filth and poverty. The world was a big place. Wherever this was, I had to get away and find my way home. But then I would glance at the sky … that red alien expanse made it clear; home was no longer a place I could hope to see again.

Alex pulled the trike next to a structure that stood out as impressive in this sea of cast-off scrap. The entire building had been constructed out of crushed cars, compacted into the shape of oversized building blocks. Even the front door was fashioned out of an old car door. Something about the place made me feel at ease, though I couldn't pin down why. Maybe I was glad to see something that didn't make me want to tuck tail and run.

"This is Hula Harry's." Alex slung her leg off the trike and held the bike in place while I stepped out of my position in the rear basket. "It's a safe spot. We hang out here a lot."

"We, as in you and I?" I pointed from her to me and back again.

She raised an eyebrow. "Yeah. Do me a favor and try not to say anything insulting. I'm your only friend right now, and you need a friend to steer you away from the considerable amount of trouble you can get caught up in around here."

I held up my hands. "I just wanted to clarify what sort of crowd I hung out with."

Alex eyed me.

"I apparently hang with a colorful hair crowd." I pointed at her blue hair and smiled.

Alex rolled her eyes and headed for the door. "Come on. I'm sure you have lots of questions that don't have anything to do with my hair."

"Actually, you're right," I said, following her toward the building. "Why can I remember things like: not all people have blue hair and the fact that I should not be able to talk to a duck, but I can't remember my own name? And what's with the people here? They're all dressed for a night in the Antarctic."

"Memory loss from the pools is different for everyone," Alex said. "Some remember nothing at all. Some come back with scattered details that don't make any sense. As for the people here, they aren't people, at least not anymore. They're Woebegone. Lost souls like you and me, except we have an advantage they don't."

I was about to ask what the advantage could possibly be

when Quack poked his head out of the backpack, making me jump away from Alex.

"What?" He broadcasted into my mind. "It was stuffy in there."

I shook my head. "Fine, how about this one. Why can I talk to a duck?"

Alex chuckled. "You don't want to start with some easier questions? Like where are you, how did you get here, why were you naked in the middle of a festering pool with no memories of your past life?"

I nodded. "Yes, all of those too. And where is this place? I'm not buying the whole dead and gone to Hell sto –"

Alex came to a sudden halt the moment we walked through the door. It took me a second to register why she had stopped. We were not the only ones who had pulled up short. Everyone in the bar had their attention focused on three hulking men who loomed over one less than impressive looking bartender.

"There a problem here?" Alex marched straight toward the three bruisers.

I reached to stop her from committing ritual suicide, but it was too late. She was already too far away.

The three guys snapped their heads around, ready to bark off a retort but as soon as they saw her, the bruisers bit back their reply.

"Just a little misunderstanding," the bartender said. He was a diminutive man in a thin short sleeve button-up and a receding hairline. "I was explaining that our supply line here at Hula Harry's is already secure. We won't be needing any help with … protection."

"Maybe you haven't heard," Alex said. "Hula Harry's is under our protection. You can address any misunderstandings to me."

The bruisers' eyes locked on me in unison. I seriously

considered backpedaling out the door fast enough to take the hinges along for the ride.

"I didn't know you were back, Gabe," said the guy closest to me. A scar split an ugly crooked path from his eye to this chin. "You back on the job then?"

"Actually, it's Gabriel," I corrected, raising a finger in the air.

Alex cut me off with a look, then shoved her hand into Scarface's chest. "Did I confuse you? I said take it up with me."

"Woah," I said. "Maybe we should all calm down and talk about this."

Scarface ignored us both and took another step in my direction. "I heard you were swimming in the fields. The big bad demon killer reduced to a freshie Disposable."

I took a step backward as the linebacker-sized wingmen shouldered Alex to the side and moved next to Scarface. My eyes flashed to Alex. I wasn't sure which terrified me more, the three oak-sized juggernauts craving my head or the blue-haired woman standing in raged fury behind them.

"You don't look all that tough to me," Scarface said. The rest of the bar had taken to studying fascinating aspects of their drinks or tabletops. No one was coming to my rescue in here. "I think Hula Harry's might have a new set of partners. What do you think, *Gabriel*? You want to hang with us for a while? We can have some fun and then send you back to the pools where you belong."

The countless number of disturbing possibilities I derived from that statement was staggering. I wanted nothing to do with any of them.

I itched to make a move for the door, but I wouldn't count more than three steps before Scarface and his bruisers made me the lonely pickle in a triple quarter-pound burger.

I was about to run for it anyway when Alex shrugged off her pack and held it out to the bartender. "Hold my duck."

Alex was on the first bruiser so fast he never had a chance. She grabbed his head and twisted it around in a way that would make an owl cringe. Bruiser One lay slumped on the floor before the other two knew what happened.

I watched the display of unbridled violence erupt and let out a scream that harmonized in two opposing tones, then erupted like an air raid siren spun at double speed. I clasped my hands to either side of my face and prepared to take the only logical course of action.

"Oh yeah." Quack's voice broke into my panic addled brain. "He's definitely going to run."

Alex pummeled the remaining stooges with several blows then smashed a bottle onto the bar for a makeshift weapon. Their faces were already bloodied, and if Bruiser One's status indicated anything as to Alex's intentions, things were about to get much, much worse. I didn't wait to see how the rest of the fight played out. I turned and ran out the door, hoping to find a quiet place to cower and make sense of this insane world.

CHAPTER FOUR

I pedaled until the front wheel of my stolen tricycle began to wobble with speed. I threaded and weaved through the streets as if I had done it my whole life, avoiding jagged obstacles and wayward souls. I wanted to believe that sooner or later I would see something recognizable. A mini mall, Quickie Mart, gas station … anything that suggested a normal, albeit inhospitable, civilization.

Instead, I found nothing but more shanties, catwalks and burning oil drums surrounded by trash-garbed sci-fi extras. Eyes peered at me from shadowy windows and I felt like the center attraction at an all-you-can-eat freak show. Darkness closed in, and that bizarre red sky turned a gloomy crimson, shading everything below in a blood red hue.

If I didn't find a place to recover my sanity soon, I would be stuck out here. All indicators suggested I had landed myself in more trouble than I'd been in at Hula Harry's. I pulled the handbrake on the trike, thinking I should turn around and head back to the slightly less insane bar. I shouldn't have left Alex by herself. Maybe she had survived the other two psychopaths.

Maybe she hadn't twisted their heads off like an old soda cap. Either way, if I were lucky, someone had already called S.W.A.T. or the National Guard … anyone who might be able to help me.

I squeezed harder on the brake. The front wheel let out an ear bending squeal then the lever broke off in my hand. Wonderful.

I scanned ahead and did my best to avoid oncoming pedestrians, then put my feet down. Since I didn't have shoes, using them as brakes wasn't a great option. I managed a sort of run step that slowed my breakneck speed, and after a couple-hundred yards, I slowed enough to make crashing a survivable prospect. With no other choice, I rammed the hapless trike into a pile of scrap in an echoed crash of corrugated metal.

"Yo, you alright there, Buddy?"

I turned to see a guy approaching from a shadowed alley between two shanties. He wore a passible grey suit for an everyday cubicle jockey, minus the tie. He approached at a concerned jog. The closer he got, the more his appearance turned from office worker to underside resident of the local overpass.

"That was a pretty hard fall. You need any help?"

He turned up his collar as if against the cold and crossed his arms across his chest. His face was almost as dirty as his jacket and when he smiled, he revealed rows of sickly, yellowed teeth.

I pulled myself to my feet and did my best to pretend I wasn't trying to keep my distance.

"I'm fine. Just a few scratches."

"You're lucky. That could have been a bad crash."

I nodded and the man stepped forward to help me pull the trike out of the pile of scrap metal.

"You from around here? You don't look familiar."

The question sounded innocent enough, but I detected a hint of eagerness in his voice that I didn't really understand.

"Actually, I'm sort of between homes right now. Just trying to figure that out."

"I don't mean to be indelicate, but you're obviously a little more than between homes." The suit eyed my bare feet. "I've been where you are, believe me, we all have. I can help you out if you want. Put you up in a safe place. Give you something to eat until you get your ..." he squinted and lowered his voice to a whisper. "Memories back."

I gawked at him. "Is it that obvious?"

He nodded. "Like I said, we've all been there. I'm sure you have a lot of questions. I'll answer anything I can. Why don't we get you inside and find something to put on your feet."

He shot me his yellowed grin and reached out to guide me forward. "I know a place right around the corner where they take care of folks like you."

I was about to thank him when a graveled voice sandblasted into my head.

"What are you doing? Alex and I circled the Gnashing Fields for weeks waiting for you, and you thank us by stealing our bike and trusting the first skuzball you run into? I'm a duck, and even I can see this guy is a Disposable dealer."

"He's not a Disposable dealer ... whatever that is," I said out loud. Quack circled above us but once I spotted him, I tried not to glance up for fear I would appear even more insane than I already had. "Go away."

The suit stopped short and turned to face me. "What was that?"

"Nothing." I pasted a smile on my face. "Just talking to myself."

The suit shook his head. His face was not so friendly anymore and he looked like he was heading back to grab me. I stepped away and he slowed his advance, regaining his more jovial demeanor.

"Sorry. Did I hear you say Disposable dealer? I don't know where you heard that, but it's a bad thing to say around here." His voice grew a little louder. "Where'd you hear that?"

I resisted the urge to locate Quack overhead. Suddenly, I

wasn't so eager to follow this guy into the darkened hollows of his home. "I'm not sure where I heard it. Just a term someone was throwing around. Maybe I should head off. I have some people waiting for me …"

The suit grinned, but this time it was in no way friendly. "No, you don't. You have no one waiting for you, and even if you did, you have no idea who they are." He marched toward me, closing the few steps between us in a fraction of a second to grab my arm. "You're coming with me. We'll have you prepped and ready to go out this evening."

I didn't know what that meant, but I did not like the sound of it. Fear surged through me as I yanked myself away, but he pulled a Dundee style knife from behind his back and held it to my throat.

"Let's not make this messy. It would be a shame to mess up that pret–"

Before he could finish the sentence, a flurry of black feathers accosted his face. The suit let go of me and swung with his free arm. When that didn't dislodge the flapping assault, he swiped at Quack with his miniature broadsword.

Something inside me snapped. The thought that this man might somehow hurt this duck was beyond unthinkable. Rage swapped seats with my fear and infused my every thought and action. I seized the suit's knife wrist and jerked him toward me, knocking Quack out of the way with my other hand. With the duck clear of danger, I twisted the suit's arm, bent his elbow back and leveraged his weight against my body until I felt his shoulder pop. He dropped the knife in a sudden screech of pain and I released him, following my assault with a targeted forward kick more designed to gain distance than do any damage.

The flurry of violence happened in a matter of seconds and I had no idea where I learned any of those moves. I staggered backward a couple of steps and stared at my hands. The rage had vanished along with my inexplicable knowledge of Kung Fu Super Strikes. Unfortunately, my continued need for said knowledge laid in an angry heap on the ground.

"You," the suit half screamed, half growled. "You dislocated my shoulder."

He twisted his body so he could find his feet without using his bad arm.

"Yeah, but you were going to hurt my duck."

My duck? What was I thinking?

That hesitation gave the suit just enough time to lunge forward. Not at me, but for his fallen knife. The guy turned out to be far more nimble than I had originally given him credit, considering his flailing assault with Quack.

Then again, grace was hard with a flapping duck on your face.

The suit rolled onto his good shoulder, swept up the knife and was on his feet, head down in a full-on charge. I stood like an innocent puppy frozen in fear when I heard a raspy whirring hiss.

The suit lurched within two steps of me when the expression on his face changed from fury, to confusion, to pain, all in the span of a millisecond. His legs stopped working and he fell to the ground in two gory bisected pieces. It was as if he had been cut in half at the waist by a giant logging saw.

I stared at him in wide-eyed horror, then turned to the side and threw up all over the ground.

"Gabe, are you all right?"

I wiped my mouth and straightened, half expecting to see Alex from Hula Harry's. Instead, I saw nothing but black leather and fire engine red hair rushing toward me, arms extended, ready to catch me if I passed out. I thought about taking her up on the offer.

"It's Gabriel."

"What?" she put her arms down.

"My name is Gabriel."

"What are you talking about? Gabriel? Are you ok?" The red-haired woman wore a mask of concern. Following close behind her came someone else. She was a muscular Latina with a shockingly normal black ponytail. She carried something like a bullwhip, but it moved and sounded nothing like its similar counterpart. It trailed behind her and seemed to slither and writhe on its own while emitting the metallic rasp of a million metal serpents sniffing out their next meal.

"Did that guy hurt you?" Red patted down my body as she rapid-fired her questions. "Where is Alex? How long have you been back? Do you have your memories?"

The Latina stood watch behind Red like a secret service agent protecting the president.

I pushed Red away and kept my eye on the Latina hoping she wouldn't offer me the same treatment she imparted on the suit.

"Excuse me, but do I know you?"

That stopped all the questions and drew matching wry smiles. Something inside me said they were both considering a sarcastic, if not comical reply.

"Yes, we know you, *Gabriel*. This is Jazzy," Red said. "And I'm Meg. We're friends. I thought another of our friends was waiting for you to get … out."

Quack waddled up behind me and drew their attention, furthering their confusion.

"You can tell them we picked you up at the Gnashing Fields but you bolted like a newborn calf." Quack grated into my mind. "They're friends. You can trust them."

"Alex and I got … separated." I managed to hold my composure for about three seconds, then all but collapsed to the ground. "I have no idea what's going on. Everyone is killing each other, there's a talking duck, no one has normal hair … please help me."

Meg and Jazzy's expressions melted into a mask of care and concern. "We've got you, Boss. Let's get you home and then Meg can go for Alex. Grab your duck and your tricycle and everything will feel better in the morning."

21

CHAPTER FIVE

—————

Much as I wished it to be so, the next morning did not bring feelings of relief and normalcy.

"Is this really necessary?" I held up our wrists where Alex had shackled us together with a pair of hot pink handcuffs. "And don't you have any in a normal color?" I let our arms fall to our sides and swing in unison as we walked to some undisclosed location.

She turned her head and shot me a grin. "First, *Gabriel*." Alex said my name in a long, drawn-out whisper that made my skin tingle. "You never complained about the color before." She winked and I swallowed hard trying figure out if she was serious or not. "And as long as you insist on running away like an angry toddler at a petting zoo, the cuffs stay on."

To be fair, I had freaked out no less than three times during our question-and-answer session last night. We spent the entire time inside some sort of reinforced Conex container that Alex, Meg and Jazzy all claimed was my shop. It wasn't like any shop I remembered. To me, a shop had shelves, aisles, fluorescent lights, the occasional screaming child and a cashier who chewed gum with her mouth open and avoided eye contact. The hollowed-out bomb crater, otherwise known as my shop, was stocked with a six pack of Dr. Pepper and three Twinkies which were all hidden in a back room. My first freak-out came when I suggested we break open the stash and have a snack. I thought all three of them were going to kill me.

The rest of the night continued pretty much like that. I would ask a simple question: Where are we? They would answer with a remarkably disturbing answer that didn't soothe my frayed nerves: You're dead in the depths of Hell, a place we call The Nine. You can never escape, and everyone here will try to hurt, cheat, molest, rape, rob or kill you … again."

How could anyone blame me for trying to run. Even the duck was hostile, and he was supposed to be some sort of twisted soul-bonded spirit animal who saved my life. I still didn't understand that one all the way. Needless to say, the myriad of explanations continued and never got better, thus my current predicament of strolling through the deviant infested streets of The Nine handcuffed to a blue-haired, tattooed supermodel with hot-pink handcuffs. An invitation for harassment to every criminal in sight.

"You never did answer my question about why I'm in Hell to begin with?" I narrowed my eyes at her. "And what about you? What got you here?"

She stopped walking and turned toward me. "Gabe, I gave you—"

"Gabriel."

She sucked in a deep breath and forced a smile. "*Gabriel,* I shared a lot of stuff with you last night. I didn't want to burden you with too much. We can discuss the details of our lives and why we're here another time. Let's just say we both made some bad choices and are doing what we can to atone for them in our afterlife."

My arm jerked forward as she took off at a more brisk speed.

"Fine." I matched her pace. "Can you at least tell me where we're going?"

Quack poked his head out of Alex's backpack, as if we needed another reason to draw attention. Apparently live waterfowl was not a thing in The Nine. He glared at me with his beady black eyes.

"If you keep whining like this, I am going to come out of this flap and dive bomb a thick wet one right into the center of your forehead. And I thought Millennials were bad."

Alex laughed as I fell back a step to sulk. She jerked me forward by our handcuffs and forced me to keep pace. "Take it easy, Mayflower. You're going to have to toughen up a little if you're going to hang around with us. I saved the best news for last."

That perked me up a little and I hardly noticed the group of Woebegone who snickered as we walked by.

"You mean there's some good news in this horrible place? I can't believe you held out on me. What is it?"

Alex smiled and nodded her head forward. I followed her gaze and saw the first real structure I had seen since waking up in this landscape of hodgepodge sheet metal and sadness. Six glass-clad towers arranged in graduating height, reminding me of a spiral staircase ... without the stairs or the safety rails. In a place like The Nine, the gleaming edifice looked like corporate heaven.

"What's that?" I stopped and stared.

Alex grinned at my obvious astonishment. "That is where we have the privilege of working. You and I are Judas Agents."

She waited for that to sink in for a second then seemed to realize that meant about as much to me as fractional differential equations.

She let out a sigh and gave me a little tug at the wrist. "Come on. You should be excited. Very few earn this distinction, and it comes with some pretty huge perks."

My eyebrows shot up. "Like what?"

"For instance, they give us a safe place to live, not to mention a reputation that keeps most lowlifes off our backs."

"That's a good thing."

Alex nodded. "And have you noticed how everyone here seems to be freezing all the time?"

"Yeah, you never did answer my question about that."

"They look cold because they are. It's an eternal torment here. Like never getting full when you eat or not getting drunk when you drink."

"Woah, we can't get drunk? What the heck were we doing at that bar … Dancing Betty's?"

"Hula Harry's," she scoffed. "It's a safe place to sit and have the kind of drink you can't find here very often, like those sodas you were so eager to slam down last night."

"Hula Harry's didn't seem all that safe to me." I annunciated the name in a disappointed pouty drawl, drawing a stare from Quack.

"Do it one more time and I swear, splat, right between the eyes."

"Fine. Calm down already." I returned my attention to Alex and tried not to dwell on the fact that I was being bullied by a duck. "Tell me about the cold thing."

"That's just it. Judas Agents don't feel that eternal chill. Everyone else in The Nine will forever try to get warm, but the cold comes from inside. A tormenting bone chilling frost that never goes away. Agents are spared that torture, and that alone is worth protecting your position at all costs, believe me."

I nodded, having never felt, or at least remembered, the chill. It was hard to relate, but it sounded terrible.

"So, what do we do at the Judas Agency? Are we some sort of secret spy organization?"

Alex nodded. "Pretty close. The agency is known affectionately as the Disaster Factory, although I wouldn't use the name around anyone in or around that building. It is the largest and most effective terrorist organization the world has *never* heard of."

I felt my face go white at the prospect.

"You mean we cause horrible things to happen…" I raised my arm, forgetting for a moment it was cuffed to hers and pointed toward the reddish sky, "up there?"

Alex did not smile or look at me as she nodded her head.

"No." I stopped walking, jerking her to a halt. "I'm not doing that."

"Okay, that's it." Quack began to wriggle his way out of his backpack. "Bombs away."

"Hold your bombing." Alex snapped and then fixed her eyes on me. "Now, you listen up. I know you don't have any memory of this place, but you can believe me when I say this place is pretty much intolerable in the best of conditions. You lose your spot at the Agency, and the best you can hope for are round trips between getting murdered and languishing in the Gnashing Fields."

"I don't care. This is where I draw the line. I'm not going to be someone who brings this kind of horror to the people living in the real world. They have enough to cope with as it is."

Alex glared at me for a moment before her expression softened. She let out a little chuckle. "I guess it's good to see something about your personality is still the same."

She nodded me forward. When I resisted, she tugged and I complied, walking slower and talking much quieter than before.

"Truth be told, you were always a bit of a pain when it came to missions. You wanted to be a do-gooder and stop things from happening rather than doing our job." She considered me a moment and smiled. "You always got me to do it with you too. I don't know how, but somehow you always convinced me to go along with your crazy schemes."

That made me smile.

"Did they work?"

"Almost never. In fact, they usually made things worse, but in the end, everything worked out. You were always sort of charmed that way."

I lost a bit of my smile.

"What's wrong?"

"What if that charm disappeared with my memory. What if all we do is the bad stuff now?"

Alex snorted. "If only I could have it so easy. Besides, you've infected me with your Johnny-do-good routine. I'm working on something a little off the books right now, and I think you might be on board."

She pepped up her step and together we strode toward the Agency with purpose.

"What is it? Are we going to slip in as double agents and stop other Judas agents from enacting some horrible catastrophe?"

Something about that statement set alarm bells off in my head so loud I clamped my mouth shut, although I had no idea why. Alex didn't seem to notice. She just marched us toward the front doors of the hulking complex.

"There's a lot going on Topside right now. A lot of bad stuff. I'm not completely sure, but you told me something right before you ... you know, died."

I nodded, urging her on. "What did I say?"

"We were fighting this ... thing up there. A Horseman."

"You mean like a guy on a horse or one of the *actual* Horsemen?"

I secretly prayed for the former.

"You're faster on the uptake than either of us were the first time around. Before you died, you told me it was the Horseman, War. You said not to fight her. She was too strong."

"Wait, her? And are all the Horsemen up there?"

"Don't be sexist, and I don't know. That is sort of what I've been working on. Let's go inside and I'll show you. There is one other thing I should tell you, though."

I braced myself for just about anything. Rabid kittens, stabbing bunnies, clowns …

"You've been suspended. You can't get caught inside the building or our supervisor might literally bite your head off."

CHAPTER SIX

"How did I get suspended?" I tugged a worn Yankees baseball hat over my head and did my best to infuse a sense of stern indigence into my voice, but somehow, it still came out like a childish complaint. I tried to convince Alex she may as well staple a *kick me* sign to my forehead as offer me a Yankees ball cap, but she wouldn't listen. She insisted I needed a *disguise,* and this hater magnet was the best she had.

We boarded an elevator big enough to fit two elephants with obesity issues and waited to get off on the floor to Alex's office.

"You committed …" I lowered my voice to a barely a whisper even though we were the only two people inside the mirrored cab. "Murder just yesterday, and I'm the one suspended? I'm almost afraid to ask what I did."

"First of all, that was self-defense, or at least in your defense. Those guys were going to fill you so full of holes you could strain noodles. And this is the Judas Agency, AKA the Disaster Factory? Killing isn't exactly off the options menu unless you try to kill a fellow agent or something. Even then, if you have a good reason …"

She looked as if she had more to say on the subject but didn't want to elaborate, and I wasn't sure how much I wanted to know. I was beginning to view Alex with a different set of eyes. If she were capable of this kind of violence it was good I never tried to strong-arm her. My own appendages may have gotten twisted into very interesting positions.

"So, what did I do that was so much worse than … murder?" I couldn't bring myself to say the word without whispering it like a B-movie sidekick.

The doors to the elevator opened and I made a move to step out, but Alex barred me across the gut with our cuffed hands and forced me to stop while she peered out the door to be sure the coast was clear. Yeah, strong-arm badass, definitely not my middle name.

"Okay, let's go." She whispered and jerked me forward. The impetuous side of me resisted enough to draw an annoyed grunt from Alex. Baby badass, maybe.

"If you must know, you brought a Hellion weapon Topside and waved it all over town for anyone with a cell phone to record. Luckily everyone was either dead or too busy fighting to notice. Bringing Hellion manufactured items Topside is a severe breach of protocol. If you hadn't landed in the pools on your own, the Judas Agency would have sentenced you there themselves. I wasn't supposed to come get you or help you, and I definitely wasn't supposed to bring you here."

I held up a finger as Alex peeked around another corner, then led us into a sea of grey cubicles so large I doubted it had an end. "I have one quick question."

Alex narrowed her eyes with impatience but didn't say anything. I took a deep breath and asked, "What's a cell phone, what is Topside, why was everyone dead, what do you mean fighting, are you telling me we can go to the real world whenever we want, what are we doing here, why don't we just stay up there?"

I ran out of breath but in no way was I out of questions. Alex shook her head. "You know, eventually you are going to get your memories back and remember all of this on your own."

I blinked at her.

"Fine." She let out a heavy sigh. "A cell phone is also called an Android or—"

"Like a robot?"

She stared at me for moment. "Yes, like a tiny robot you can carry around in your pocket."

"Wow, that sounds amazing." I smiled. "I can't wait to see one."

She jerked me forward and we made our way through the endless corridors of padded grey walls. "And yes, we can go Topside, that's what we call the regular world, or the world of the living, but it's a perk of the Judas Agency and only agents can do it. Well, demons can, but they don't do it very often. It's messy. Even Lucifer is bound to this realm by some inextricable force and can't leave.

"Wow." I skip stepped to keep up with Alex's feverish pace. "I can't believe we're allowed to do something the big boss can't."

Alex shrugged. "I hear it's a pretty sore subject, but things have to get done, and we're here to do them."

"Again, why don't we stay there?"

She shivered as if reliving a memory. "Let's just say I like my body parts where they are. Keep your Topside trips short. You will not appreciate the consequences."

I nodded. "So, if you weren't supposed to fish me out of the pools, what was I supposed to do all alone out there?"

"If you're sentenced to the Gnashing Fields, you're on your own. The agency believes it part of your sentence to regain your memories alone. It's their way of making sure only the truly ruthless at heart make it back."

I looked over at her, narrowing my eyes in confusion.

She ignored my unvoiced question as we turned yet another

corner. The cubicles on this floor were truly endless. After a few seconds, she succumbed to my stare.

"When you come out of the Gnashing Fields, your personality is unpolluted." She sighed. "You're un-jaded by the memories of your past, so there is nothing left but who you truly are deep inside under that black hardened crust of life experience. For most, that means they become innocent again. Untarnished by the horrible things and experiences that may have made them the way they were. Some people are just nasty through and through. They're the ones the Judas Agency likes to keep. The ones that pretended to be *nice* in order to function in society."

I shuddered. "And these are the people you … we work with?"

She shrugged. "Work with, work for. Believe it or not, quite a few good ones manage to stick around. Look at us." She smiled. "I'm still here and you're back to annoying me with your infectious do-gooder personality disorder."

Alex finally pulled me into one cubicle amidst the monochrome ocean of colorless squares and pushed me into a chair beside her desk.

She sat on a chair next to me and faced some sort of glass window that didn't open to anything but darkness. I expected her to reach out to touch it, but she hesitated and turned toward me again.

"Ok, *Gabriel,* I know this is going to seem new and unbelievable and awe inspiring to you all over again, but can you hold in your wonderstruck amazement so we can skip the long explanations about how new technology works? Trust me when I say you have seen this all before and when the astonishment wears off, there is just a lot of yelling and red-faced banging when you try to make it work for yourself."

I aimed for an air of indigence, but inside I all but vibrated with childlike expectation.

"Of course. I'll remember all of this eventually, right?"

"Right." She paused another second then said. "Quack, poke your head out here a sec."

The pack on Alex's back rippled with movement, then the zipper on top opened and a feathered black head poked out of the canvas.

"What's up boss. I was just taking a break from sir-whines-a-lot."

Alex chuckled. "I'm about to turn on this computer. If he gets all wide-eyed and handsy, bite him."

"Hey."

"I'm on it. I will latch on like a baby crocodile … for a can of those mustard sardines."

Alex made a sour face but nodded. "I don't know how you eat those things."

"Pressure sealed heaven."

"I resent the fact that you think I have so little self-control that you need to —"

My words were cut abruptly short when the dark window burst into colorful projections so clear I felt as if I could touch them. Alex began an intricate series of gestures with her free hand, causing videos and pictures that seemed almost 3D to appear before my eyes. I wanted her to slow down so I could appreciate it. Watch and … touch.

I reached out with my un-cuffed hand, extending a finger like Michelangelo's David.

"Sardines here I come."

I managed to jerk away just in time to save my digit from Quack's dirty duck beak.

"Dang it," he squawked and let out a frustrated honk. "I thought I had you for sure. Look at the screen again. Isn't it amazing? Did you know anything you touch will materialize in real life?"

"Quack!"

"What, really?" I reached for the screen, but this time Alex slapped my hand away.

"Aw come on," Quack said. "I deserve those sardines."

"Knock it off, and no this is not a magic materializer."

Just as well, since the image on the screen had been a M-1 Abrams tank.

"Pay attention and keep your hand to yourself." She pointed to a series of videos on the screen. "This is what's happening Topside in the United States right now."

A montage of battles between a mix of military, police and regular civilian forces flashed across the screen. I didn't have any memory of my life, but I did recognize the world. At least what I thought it should be. Now it was war torn, battle worn and burning. There were crying children, bloodied soldiers and dead bodies littered everywhere. Even with no memories to pull from, I knew it was one of the most terrifying things I had ever seen.

Nothing showed on the screen that would make me want to touch it now.

"How did this happen? Was it … I mean, I don't remember it being …"

I couldn't form a coherent thought.

"No, you never saw Topside like this," Alex said. "Everything here happened because of one thing."

She made another gesture with her hand, and the video on the screen changed. The living embodiment of death almost galloped off the screen in my direction. A huge figure on horseback wearing archaic red battle armor wielded a broken broadsword made of pure obsidian. The horseman peered directly at me from the screen. My muscles froze as horror infused every cell in my body. I had no specific recollection, but flashes of fire, pain, fear and death overwhelmed my vision until I was hardly aware of my surroundings. I couldn't breathe. I had to get away. Had to run. This thing meant to kill me. Screen or no screen, it would cleave me, cranium to crotch.

I stood and jerked away, yanking backward with all my might. I couldn't form a single word, but I was vaguely aware of the moaning little screams that escaped my lips.

"Don't worry," Quack said. "I got this one."

I toppled my chair and wrenched Alex back by our hand-cuffed arms.

"Oops." Quack amended. "Maybe I don't got this one. You may have to hold him down while I bite him."

Alex made a sweeping gesture with her free hand and the screen went blank as she staggered out of her own chair. It took her a couple of steps to right herself, but she managed to keep her feet. By then I was already stretched outside the cubicle, free arm in front of me, pulling for all I was worth.

"All right, it's over. Calm down."

I kept pulling, my wide eyes locked on the blank screen as if it might come to life and spew forth the instrument of my gruesome death.

Alex put a hand on my cheek and forced me to look into her eyes. The feel of her fingers sent a warm electric surge through my body I didn't quite understand, but I it was enough to make me abandon my terror-stricken retreat.

"I'm sorry." She kept her voice smooth, calm and apologetic. "I shouldn't have done that without warning you. I hoped the shock of seeing the Horseman might bring back your memories. Sometimes it works to face the moment of your death. I promise I won't do it again."

"I don't ever want to see that monster again. We can't fight that. That thing is horrible."

Alex's hand fell to my chest and more electric fire ran through my bones, making me wonder if there was more to our partnership than being partners. Something told me this wasn't the right time to ask, but I wasn't all that eager for our contact to end either.

"I know that was upsetting," she whispered. Her voice

consoling but with an edge of warning now. "But remember where you are and watch what you say."

I took a moment to breathe and then nodded. "Okay. I'm alright. Sorry. Just don't bring that thing back."

"I won't, I promise. At least not without telling you or getting your permission first."

I nodded and she turned to lead us into the cubicle, holding my cuffed hand on her shoulder.

The comforting gesture lasted only a second before a painful pinch bit into the side of my hand.

"Got 'em! You can pay me as soon as we get Topside, thank you."

I pulled my hand away and rubbed the reddened spot on the meaty side of my palm.

"I wasn't even freaking out."

"Yeah, but you were definitely getting handsy."

Alex laughed and sat without saying anything else, leaving me to wonder a little more about my earlier thoughts.

I was about to ask, when Alex turned on the screen. Despite her promise, the possibility that the Horseman might appear made me wince, ready to bolt.

"Don't worry," she said, seeing my apprehension. "I'm just looking up a little information on someone else. You're right about War. She's way too powerful to fight, even with both of us at one hundred percent. I tried a few things to slow her down while you were away. I hacked into the news and social media to talk things down from the outside."

"Social what?"

She chuckled. "Never mind. By the time I explain the Internet, you'll have your memories back."

I visibly sulked a little but decided not to press further.

"My plan worked for a while," she continued. "At least until the outlets caught on that their news copy had changed right before it hit the presses. The video prompts on live television broadcasts were the most fun to mess with. I could alter the questions reporters asked those witless politicians and they would just stare in baffled amazement when they related to real problems rather than boosted ratings."

Alex scrolled through a few more screens and seemed to take note of a specific image I did not recognize.

"Other things didn't work out so well. I intervened with battlefield orders a few times, but that hit too close to home. War had a tight hold on her troops. No matter what I did, she canceled any order to stand down."

"Let me get this straight," I said. "That scary woman is actually War. As in the Horseman War, and she's running around making the world fight and kill each other?"

"Actually, she initially confined herself to the North American continent, but now it looks like she's taking her campaign south. I've seen reports of fighting in Mexico and South America, although not nearly as intense. I'm not sure if War is triggering the conflicts directly, or if it's just spill over from the U.S."

"What about the rest of the world. What are they doing about it?"

"Funny enough, they don't seem to care all that much. For all the times the U.S. involved itself and helped with foreign affairs, the rest of the world seems quite content to let the U.S. work this out all by themselves."

Alex turned off her screen and stood, pulling me up with a gentle tug of her hand.

"That is where I think you and I can do a little ..." She lowered her voice and leaned into me to whisper, "good."

She leaned back and shot me a wink.

"If I'm right, there are supposed to be four of those jokers running around, but War is the only one who has gained any real power. If we intervene early with the others, maybe we can stop ..."

She paused as I shook my head. "Stop what? Stop an apocalypse?"

She shrugged. "Yeah. I figure we have to try."

I laughed. "Won't we get into trouble if we're caught?"

Alex's expression turned flat and annoyance crept into her eyes.

"I need you to make up your mind here. Are you on board to help, or would you rather stand by while millions of innocent people die? I can wait while you figure it out."

I let out a breath and looked around, not missing the irony of her raised voice after telling me I needed to keep my voice down.

"I'll help, of course," I whispered. "But what if we're caught?"

"If we get caught, we will have to hope Quack survives and can somehow fish us out of the Sulfur Pools all by himself because no one else will help us. I'm not going to lie to you. This is dangerous on about every possible level, but whether you remember or not, you are the one who infected me with this conscience, and I am not about to run this gauntlet alone."

I shook my head. "I can't believe I was on board with doing stuff like this."

"Right now, that makes two of us. Go with the flow and pretend you know what you're doing. Maybe that will be enough to keep you out of trouble."

I nodded. "All right. What do we do next?"

Alex smiled. "We're going Topside. It's finally time for us to visit an old friend, and I for one am ready to have that conversation up close and personal."

CHAPTER SEVEN

Alex pulled a handcuff key out of her pocket while we rode the oversized elevator down to the main floor of the building.

"I'm going to take these off." She held our arms up together and stared me straight in the eye. "No more running. I can't have you taking off every time something spooks you, but being shackled at the wrist raises too many questions."

She worked the tiny key and the ratcheted links fell free, allowing her to catch the cuffs in her free hand like she had practiced the trick a thousand times.

"I want you to promise you won't bolt or I'll have to take you to your shop and lock you up until you get your head straight."

The thought of staying in that dingy hollow even one more day was enough to keep me from running. Besides, I was eager to see what my apartment at the agency looked like. Considering what I had seen of the building so far, I had a feeling it was pretty nice.

"Don't worry. I'm over the initial shock. I promise I won't run." I rubbed at my wrist while Alex put the cuffs in her back pocket. "You've told me about everything already." I smiled. "What else could make me want to run and hide?"

The elevator doors slid open, and there stood an eight-foot monster, waiting for us on the ground floor.

Clad in armor, man muscle and animal fur, the beast had the head of a lion and a pair of dusky brown wings that dragged the ground at his back. My Yankees baseball hat disguise didn't slow him for a second. As soon as he laid eyes on me, the creature bared his teeth in a snarl and snatched me out of the elevator, hoisting me into the air by my shoulder.

"Put the cuffs back on, put the cuffs back on." I screeched in a tiny voice as my feet windmilled in a cartoon sprint.

"Sabnack." Alex popped out of the elevator almost as fast as I did, except she did so under her own power. "We were just about to come see you."

Her tone suggested she spoke anything but the truth.

"Gabe made it back, as you can see. We were just on our way to give you the good news."

The half man, half monster continued to hold me aloft with one hand causing my shoulder no small amount of pain. I let out a whimper and grasped at his wrist to alleviate some of the pressure.

"Please, Sir. Could you let go? This really hurts."

Sabnack shifted his gaze from me to Alex.

"Sir?"

Quack's voice broke into my mind from within Alex's back-pack. He had retreated to avoid being spotted at the agency, but I could still hear him in my head.

"The old Gabe doesn't say, Sir. You better grow a pair if you don't want to become a demon squeezy toy."

"Take it easy, you oversized house cat," I said. "It was a joke. Don't the zookeepers hand out a sense of humor at the lion exhibit?"

I stole a look at Alex for any indication that my acting job landed anywhere near the ballpark. Her mouth just hung open. I was beginning to question the nature of Quack's friendship. The fact that he laughed uncontrollably inside my head was a pretty good clue.

"That was perfect," he cackled. "Keep being a smart ass. He loves that. We're all going to laugh about this later, I promise."

Something about my statement must have rung true because the beast let go of my shoulder and I landed hard on my feet, almost buckling at the knees.

"You are forbidden from interfering with his reintegration process." His voice boomed in the large hallway while other agents and workers buzzed around as if we were a permanent feature in the room.

"Of course," Alex said. "He found me. I was in my office when he showed up. Must have been a short turn around somehow."

She smiled and looked at me. It took me a moment to realize she was waiting for me to say something, anything to convince him I wasn't one slice shy of a pizza.

"Yeah, it's good to see you Sad Snack."

Quack burst into laughter again.

Alex palmed her face.

The beast eyed us both and then leaned forward to sniff me.

"He even smells of sulfur. He's two days fresh if he's a moment."

"Come on, *Sabnack*." Alex annunciated his name a little more slowly for my benefit. "I need my partner. He's up and out, that's all that matters. Look at it this way, you don't have to find someone else to put up with me. Less headache for you and considering the shape he's in, more headache for me. It's pretty much a win, win."

Sabnack looked to me and seemed to consider. I did my best to look somehow confident and humble at the same time. I think I came across more like a quivering chihuahua.

"Fine, but keep him on a leash. If this comes back to me, I will make it my mission to ensure your return trip to the Gnashing Fields is slow, painful and full of teeth."

He bared his huge canines at me in a snarl as if to punctuate whose teeth would do the gnashing.

"Got it." Alex grabbed me by the arm and started to pull me away.

"Thank you, Nap Sack. You won't regret this. I won't let you down."

Another hail of laughter imposed itself into my thoughts, and Alex pulled harder before the huge lion beast had a chance to change his mind.

CHAPTER EIGHT

"I see you haven't lost your touch with the landings."

My head spun as I struggled to make sense of the sky and the ground. I bent over, hands on knees, while standing in almost waist deep in water. It took every bit of concentration I had to not hurl an Exxon Valdez spill all around me.

"Get out, before someone calls the cops."

I looked up to see Alex motioning me to the edge of the huge fountain I resided in. A twin to another that stood at the opposite edge of the park. It had low, white stone walls, a blue tile interior and a gorgeous water feature in the middle. If I weren't standing in the basin looking like a homeless lunatic taking a bath, I would have appreciated its elegance and simple beauty.

"Hold on. Don't go anywhere."

I felt Quack scramble out of my new backpack like a crack addict fighting for his last hit on earth. "I never get a chance to swim. I'm a duck. I want in."

He splashed into the noisy fountain as I scrambled toward the edge.

"You could have given me a little more warning." I sloshed

to the side and threw my leg over the wall with a *schlunk* of water.

We had changed into different clothes for our trip Topside. Alex wore a long coat and tall boots over her t-shirt and jeans. I wore a skintight brown and orange Gore-tex outfit with hiking boots. The urban catastrophe looked ridiculous, but she said I always insisted on wearing it before I lost my memories. If the patchwork ensemble said anything about my idea of a good look, I never wanted that part of my memory back.

"I told you to picture where you wanted to land. And I also told you to stay away from water." Alex grabbed me by my arm and made a point of yanking me the rest of the way out of the fountain. "Water will kill you," she hissed at me in loud whisper.

"You said raaaainnnnnn waaaaaterrrrrrrr." I amended. "This stuff has been so filtered, chlorinated and processed it's classified as a synthetic element."

"You've got that right," Quack agreed. "I just pooped and it atomized into crystals."

I started to laugh but Alex balled her fist and jabbed me right in the sternum forcing me spit out my chuckle as a cough.

"I put my neck on the line for you with Sabnack. This is not a joke. I realize you're struggling right now, but there are real dangers up here. Rainwater will melt you into a puddle of engine sludge and you will feel every second of it. You may not care, but I don't want to watch that happen again. I need you here, not in the fields. Now, get your head in the game."

"Ok. I'm sorry." I nodded. "What do you mean, again? Was I … melted by rainwater?"

"It didn't kill you but believe me when I say you were not in a happy place."

"I'll try not to let it happen again, but I didn't do it on purpose. I saw the fountain and …"

"It doesn't matter." Alex took a breath and closed her eyes for a moment.

"When she's like this, it's best to shut up and stay out of fist range." Quack continued to paddle around the fountain with glee.

"I could have used the fist advice a few seconds earlier."

"With Alex, that's good advice most of the time."

When she opened her eyes, Alex looked a little more centered and less murdery. "Look, I'm sorry I got so angry. I know you're still trying to figure things out, but you have to pay attention and follow my lead. We're immune to many things up here, but others will kill you fast. I only want to keep you safe. Let's move and I'll fill you in on more of the details as we go."

I nodded and looked around, surveying the area for the first time. It was a beautiful morning. Brisk sunshine with a slight breeze skittering leaves along the concrete. The huge open park was so much nicer than the Hell-hole we called home. The two large water features dominated the center area, but a towering pillar topped with a masculine sculpture adorned the far end. Below the figure, gleaming gold lions stood sentry on all four corners. The park looked like a place that should have been teeming with thousands of people, but only a handful were present.

"What is this place?" I held my arms away from my body and kept my legs spread hoping to drain off as much water as possible.

"This is Trafalgar Square. There are usually tons of people here, so I was hoping we could blast into existence out of nowhere and everyone would freak out when they saw us land." She eyed me, her comment dripping with sarcasm. "Too bad I arrived in the old police box on the southeast corner of the park where I told you to appear and popped out all inconspicuous."

"I said I was sorry."

Alex shook her head.

"Looks like your people theory is shot too. No one's here."

She surveyed the smattering of people scattered throughout the park.

"I heard the British government quarantined most of the country after that last smallpox outbreak, but I had no idea people were this isolated."

I raised an eyebrow at her.

"Short story long, an old acquaintance from the agency, Simeon Scott, horned in on one of our assignments and hijacked the body of a very sweet and also very smart nanotechnology scientist named Ryan Rokuda. He used his tech as a sort of bio cure here in the UK when a mysterious outbreak of smallpox threatened the entire country. I think Simeon set the whole thing up in order to release his nano technology and infect as many people with his nanites as possible, although I'm not sure why."

Understanding began to dawn on me as Alex explained more and more about the sick and infected and this man Simeon who seemed to be behind it all.

"His technology potentially saved the lived of millions. In turn millions have also been vaccinated with Simeon's nanites and I, for one, am waiting for that other shoe to drop. What is he planning to do? Millions of people now carry the nanites. What will he do with the nanites now that they're inside their hosts? How will the nanites affect them? If he wanted to make people sick, why not let the smallpox epidemic run its course?"

"You think this guy Simeon might become another Horseman don't you."

Alex smiled and shot me a wink.

"You know, you're pretty quick for a guy who has no memories."

"Yeah." Quack paddled over to the edge of the fountain looking positively elated. "I think I like him better this way. More brains, less clutter."

Alex chuckled. "I still want the old Gabe back, but you're

not too bad for now." She put a hand on my shoulder and smiled.

"Gee, thanks." My entire body flushed with heat the moment she touched me, but I tried to ignore it. Something about the way she looked at me made me wonder again if we had something more than a work partnership. "So, are we…" I pointed back and forth between us. "I mean, are you and I …"

"Are you asking if we're together? A couple?"

"Yeah." I nodded.

She shrugged then ran her finger down my cheek. "What do you want the answer to be?"

"Um … I'm … I don't …"

She laughed. "Come on, Cowboy. Let's go." She took my hand, pulling me along. "The building Simeon used as company headquarters is only a few blocks away. Simeon dropped off the radar a couple of weeks ago, but I want to visit and see what we can find out."

Quack groaned on my head. "Can't I stay and swim a little longer. I'm filthy as a pigeon. If any of my friends saw me like this, I would never hear the end of it."

"Just catch up." I laughed without turning to look at him. "You have wings. You can fly over when you're done."

Memories or no, I knew he wouldn't let us get far. The soul bond we shared not only allowed us to talk, it made sure any separation felt more than a little uncomfortable. Every time I moved more than a few feet away from him, anxiety crept into my brain. Small at first, but before I knew it, I'd be scrambling to find him as if my life depended on it, and according to Alex, it did. Quack felt the same way. Our link would send him flying after me before I was out of sight.

"Perfect." Quack flapped water onto his wings and gazed at the sun. I felt a little guilty for walking away while he clearly enjoyed a state of bliss, but Alex and I had more important things to take care of. Like saving the world.

"So, which direction?"

Alex looked around and took a heading past the huge lion statues at the front of the park. "That way."

I leveled a hand in that direction to indicate ladies first, and we started walking. We weren't to the first golden lion before trouble stepped into our path.

CHAPTER NINE

An eclectic looking woman stepped in front of us, blocking our way. She wore a black navy pea coat and had stark white hair and eyebrows so bright they could have come straight out of a crayon box. The moment she saw us, she threw her arms wide as if she expected us to greet her with a hug.

"Greetings fellow outworlders. How goes the fight?"

I smiled and stepped forward to hug this new arrival thinking she must be a friend, but Alex snatched me by my collar and drew me back.

"I thought I told you to stop tracking us."

The woman continued to hold out her hands, wiggling her fingers in a tempting welcome for a few more seconds then let her arms fall when Alex didn't take the bait.

"How else am I supposed to see you. It's not like I can call or pop by your office. I wanted to say hello and see how you're doing. There are so few of us here. Why can't we be cordial?"

"Because you show up only when there's trouble and then you do nothing but sit back and watch. Forgive me if I don't like being your sideshow entertainment."

The woman pushed out her lower lip in a ridiculous show of

mock sadness. "That's not fair. You know I can't interfere in company business. I just want someone to talk to. Besides, you have to admit, I have helped you sometimes."

"Excuse me." I smiled. "I probably know this already, but tell me your name again?"

The woman looked from me to Alex and back.

Alex nodded. "Yeah. Thanks to your *help*, he died the last time we were here. Not that you care or can even comprehend what he went through, but the torture of the Gnashing Fields—"

"Wipes his memory away for a little while." The woman clapped her hands in front of her chest. "How fun."

Alex clenched a fist and seemed primed to end this woman's glee in a blinding flurry of violence. Considering how she handled the three hulking goons the other night at Hula Harry's, I shuddered to think what she might do to this one woman.

Thankfully our guest seemed to key in on her impending doom and held out her hands in placation.

"I didn't mean the part about him dying of course. Just the time of discovery. I mean, how often do we get to return to that time in our youth when everything around us is so fascinating and new?"

"More like dark and terrifying," I answered. "But yeah, I guess some things are pretty cool to see again for the first time."

Alex rolled her eyes. I sensed I was being set up for something but didn't know what.

"I am Samyaza." The woman held out her hand in greeting and I took it. "My friends call me Sammy. I am an angel."

My jaw fell slack open, and I stopped shaking her hand.

Sammy's smile broadened at my obvious astonishment.

I stood for a moment, unmoving then stepped back, releasing her hand. I averted my eyes to the ground and began to kneel.

Before I made it halfway down, Alex grabbed the tiny, short hairs on the back of my neck and pulled me up, making me squeak with surprise and pain. "If your knees touch the ground, I swear your lips will follow right behind them."

My eyes turned to Sammy, then Alex, who had resumed her death glare at the grinning woman.

"Are you about finished with your narcissism expedition? We have things to do."

Alex grabbed me by the hand to lead me away, but Sammy held out an arm and waylaid our advance.

"Please. I'm sorry. I was just having a bit of fun. I really did come to talk. You are in great danger here."

A homeless woman crossed my field of view behind Sammy. Other than the fact that she was one of only a few people in the park, something about her seemed odd. Nothing obvious, more covert and creepy, like the way a spider moved; slow, yet jerky whenever my eyes fell upon her. I elbowed Alex to get her attention, but she was too busy glaring at Sammy.

"We're always in danger. That's our job. We can take care of ourselves, no thanks to you."

"Not this time." Sammy shook her head. "This is different. Events are spiraling in a way they were never meant to. This isn't the right time, yet here we are. The powers involved are, if you will forgive the term, biblical, to say the least. This is not a job for a pair of rogue Judas agents. You will be cut down in the aftermath." She motioned to me by way of example. "You and I both know this is the very least of what could happen."

Alex huffed. "I find it ironic that of the three of us are standing here, it's the angel who wants us to stand aside and watch the world burn. Why is it, that an agent of all that is supposed to be good and holy, does nothing while we, Agents of Hell and Destruction, risk our necks to save the world's proverbial bacon? Is it a pork thing?"

Sammy's jovial demeanor slipped a hair and I found myself grateful that Alex had saved me from prostrating myself to this being. She was right. What kind of angel lets terrible things happen when she could do something to stop it?

"My position on this plane has not changed. Though I am here to observe, and indeed standby to act if called upon to do so, you know I'm not allowed to intercede in events that unfold among the living. To do so would disrupt my edict and corrupt freewill among humanity. I would forfeit my position and for what? To watch mankind find another cataclysmic way to end their existence? Stand aside and let events play out as they may. They will happen whether you suffer against them or not. It is not an easy or pleasant task, but the most prudent one. You are my friends. I don't want to see you hurt."

Alex huffed out a laugh. "Spoken like a true bureaucrat. Stand by and watch if you want. Just don't get in the way. Besides, I don't see much danger around here. Not unless you're worried about a lack of crowds."

The spider woman crossed my field of view, and this time she jerked her head around in a motion so unnatural it looked mechanical. Alex saw it too and stiffened with alarm.

"The danger you seek is so much larger than you know. If you can't see that, you are looking in the wrong place."

She pointed over our shoulders, and I turned in time to see Quack flapping toward us along the ground at a full on a duck sprint.

"Hey guys. We may have a little issue. Either the tour buses let out, or the guy we're looking for may have heard we're here."

Page Break

CHAPTER TEN

Alex and I turned in unison to see what could only be described as a single living organism enveloping the far end of the park. A mass of humans rolled in like a muddy wave, slow and deliberate and not at all moving in a human-like fashion. The bodies shifted and roiled, appearing and disappearing in and among one another as the tide advanced.

The pace at which they moved appeared wholly unnatural. They were not jerky or graceless as a mass of individuals should have been. Rather they advanced in a smooth, fluid, almost mechanical motion. The only anomaly to their imperfect symmetry was the single Horseman casually leading the relentless invasion.

His thick goatee and sunglasses matched the black top hat and trench coat he wore. I would have expected his horse to mirror his dark, sinister apparel, but instead his mount glowed white as the driven snow. From a distance, the animal appeared pure and majestic with its long flowing mane, but as they drew closer, the fevered look in its eyes betrayed the madness of a wild animal.

"Alex and friend. So good to see you on this fine European morning."

The man's voice had just a touch of a genteel southern drawl and every word dripped with condescension.

"I can only assume you have come to see the sights in the area. Might I suggest starting with the National Gallery. They have a fantastic exhibit featuring Jan Matejko's Copernicus."

"What are you up to Simeon?" Alex spat, ignoring the bait. "What have you done to these people?"

Simeon brought his mount to a halt, and with it, the rest of the horde behind him followed suit. The action itself was the most disturbing thing I'd seen so far. They did not stop so much as turn off. Each body froze as one in position whether mid-step, swinging an arm or turning a head. Not a single person so much as blinked. The only sound was the rasp from a thousand of wheezing throats all hissing in strained unison to keep the unified organism alive.

"These?"

Simeon motioned backward with his hand rather than visually acknowledge the horrifying apparition behind him.

"These are not people. This is my flock. A tiny fraction to be sure. I thought it prudent to bring a less intimidating number. After all we are friends."

Alex Scoffed. "We are not friends. And that doesn't answer my question."

Simeon laid a hand to his chest in mock offence. "You wound me. After all we have been through, my peach. Did we not have good times together?"

Something about his words lit a spark deep in my chest, and not the warm fuzzy kind you feel for kittens or wayward baby seals. This was the white-hot flare of anger, and I wasn't sure why. Hearing him speak to Alex that way fanned that flame into an inferno.

This man radiated pure evil. Not only had he somehow

enslaved these people, he lived inside a host body himself. Alex said he had hijacked this person, taken him over in order to *live*. What sort of monster would do that? And what happened to the man who owned that body? Was he still inside? The mere thought of such a violation made me want to help. To rescue this man from Simeon's unnatural prison.

I managed to keep my mouth shut by clenching my jaw, but my feet failed to cooperate. I stepped toward Alex to stand in solidarity with her and glared a warning at Simeon, horde or no horde.

"Oh my, the smoldering stranger to the rescue I see." He shot me a smile so patronizing I wanted to launch myself forward and tear it off his face. "Don't worry. This water is so far under the bridge I can't even see it. However, I do like to reminisce."

"Why don't you come down off that horse and I'll —"

Alex put a hand on my arm, stopping the creative expletive I was about to paint for him.

"Don't fall into his trap. He likes to swim in his charm, but it's really just a big pool of insecurity and diluted testosterone masked in a pretty vocabulary."

Simeon laughed.

"Touché my peach. You have not lost your touch. I do miss our verbal banter."

"I don't miss any of it. Now, answer … my … question."

She annunciated each and every word as if she were a mother scolding a child.

"Very well." Simeon sighed. "Though I am sure you have already guessed the answer."

He raised an eyebrow inviting the response.

"Nanites." Was the only thing Alex said.

"Correct, my peach. Self-replicating, auto propagating nanites that spread through a living population faster than any virus or bacteria. Once inside the bloodstream, they take hold of the host, overcoming the autonomic and central nervous systems.

Each poor wretch is then absorbed into my flock to do my good works upon this earth."

He spread his arms like a wayward preacher and smiled.

"As I said, this is but a fraction of our congregation. I have infected the entire European continent. So, you see, I have not simply formed an army, I have created a force of nature. An unstoppable wave as immutable as the ocean itself, ready to sweep the continent and start this planet anew."

The thought that so many had already fallen to this lunatic was almost unthinkable. If what he said were true, these people were still in there somewhere. Simeon just controlled them like a million RC robots. Their minds and souls imprisoned while he used their outward bodies as flesh covered weapons. Their thoughts and terrified feelings would be their own. Simeon had not only enslaved the body he occupied. He had enslaved this entire population. For that, Simeon deserved a fate worse than death.

Alex crossed her arms, seemingly less impacted by Simeon's grandiose description of horror and world domination.

"Fine, but why do they look like that?" She pointed and made the face of someone trapped on an elevator with a lactose intolerant milk glutton.

At first, I had no idea what she was talking about. I just saw a terrifying horde of people under Simeon's control, but when I took a closer look, I noticed something else. They were all a disgusting mass of snot and goo. A preschool Petri dish of cold and allergy sufferers without a single Kleenex to save them. It was so disgusting I couldn't help but wipe my hands on the front of my shirt in a subconscious attempt to stay clean.

"Eww." Quack commented into my mind for the first time since Simeon's arrival. "I don't know how smart it is to taunt the lunatic, but that's just gross."

I noticed Sammy still stood behind us, but true to form, she had not said a single word or made any move to interfere in the proceedings. Alex was right, for an angel she was disturbingly ineffective in the assistance department.

Simeon's posture of magnificence sagged and he turned in his creaky ivory colored saddle to look at his flock, still motionless behind him. "There are side effects to the assimilation process." Simeon's voice seemed almost sheepish. I stood awed by Alex's ability to cut this guy down a notch or two at the height of his villainous supremacy.

"Their immune system seems to react against the nanites, eliciting some minor cold and flu symptoms."

"Minor?" Alex exclaimed. "They could snot start a bobsled. This is your master plan? An army of Snot Zombies? For all your pomp and circumstance, this is your elegant weapon of mass destruction?"

She let out a laugh.

Unsure of what to do, I let out an uncomfortable chuckle of my own.

"What are you doing here?" Simeon snapped his attention to Sammy, all pretense of civility gone. "You have no business in this place. Leave us alone and do your watching somewhere else."

I found it a little surprising that Simeon knew Sammy and that he would speak to her in such a venomous tone. Then again, I had no memory of anything, so perhaps Sammy's identity was common knowledge.

"I'm simply here to observe as my edict demands, and to warn a few friends from danger if I can, nothing more."

"Then be gone angel, for the true power on this earth has work to do."

Simeon regained his stature as if speaking to the entire world. This time I doubted anything Alex could say would tear him down.

"For I am no longer Ryan Rokuda, nor Simeon Scott. I am

Pestilence. I ride to conquer my quarter of this earth and shall meet with my brethren to see the whole of humanity burn."

He turned his eyes down on us, and his maniacal smile made him look something altogether less than human.

"Take heed. The gates of Hell will overflow with the souls of the fallen. I will be the one to send them there. Starting, I think, with you."

CHAPTER ELEVEN

Any thought of reasoning our way out of this predicament flew out the window when Sammy burst into a cloud of pigeons and dive-bombed Simeon's face. He shouted in anger and frustration, and Alex wasted no time grabbing my arm to pull me away at a dead sprint in the opposite direction. Quack wasn't far behind. He took a few waddling steps and launched himself airborne, leading the escape with his flapping wings in an all-out frenzy.

"I told you not to taunt the lunatic." Quack's words fell in time with his frantic flaps. "We're always - running - because - you have - to taunt - the lunatics."

"That way." Alex pointed toward the traffic circle ahead, ignoring Quack. Stationary double-decker busses and the stereo-typical black cabs of London filled the space, although none of them were occupied or moving. "We'll never outrun them on foot." Alex panted as I followed her lead. "Get in that cab."

I did as she said, sprinting for the passenger door. I jerked it open just in time for Quack to swoop in, then dove in myself, only to realize Alex and I had made an American mistake. We were in England. Cars here drove on the left side of the road with steering wheels on the right, leaving me firmly in the driver's seat.

We looked at each other and she shook her head.

"No time. Just drive."

I fumbled across the dash and found a key in the ignition, thankful my memory somehow filled in these blanks. The engine roared to life, and I slammed the accelerator to the floor. We tore away in an unimpressive hum of power. Palms slapped against the rear of the car, making us both jump. The horde of Snot Zombies had caught up to us. I looked in my mirror to see the histamine soldiers move as one at an impossible speed considering the condensed and coordinated way they moved.

They enveloped everything in their path. Cars, park benches, posts, trash cans, even fallen Snot Zombies. They absorbed any and all obstacles within the sheer mass of numbers and kept coming, never wavering, slowing or altering course.

Alex screamed as they scaled Nelson's Column. The huge statue stood at the head of the park, and now it toppled under the sheer weight of their numbers, nearly bashing us into oblivion before we could escape the traffic circle. It was a terrifying sight and altogether hopeless in terms of standing against something so single-minded and massive; only a pittance according to what Simeon claimed he had at his command. We may have been better off facing War after all.

"Keep driving up this street but not too fast." Alex pointed ahead of us. "Keep them packed in behind us if you can."

Quack and I both turned to stare at Alex as if she had grown a third eye out of her cheek.

"You planning to go back and taunt him a little more?" Quack asked. "Because you can let me out right now."

"He's right." I swerved around a parked car and made my way through an abandoned intersection. At least I didn't have to worry about any pedestrians. "We need to get away from here, not lead them on a pleasure stroll. Are you trying to get us killed?"

"We have one way back to The Nine, and Simeon is standing on top of it. We have to get to the splice point where we came in."

The reality of her words hit me like a brick. Alex explained how the Envisage Splice elevator worked before we left. We land Topside and the return portal waits for us in the same spot. Unfortunately, my portal was currently carpeted with Snot Zombies.

"We have to assume he, or one of his minions, saw your graceless landing into the fountain. He'll have those ears to elbows full of snorting zombies, but he may not know that I came through the police box on the southeast corner of the park."

I grinned. "So, we lead them around in a big circle until the bunny trail thins enough for us to backtrack and hit *your* splice point. Genius."

I let off the accelerator and allowed the Snot Zombies to amble closer. We were three blocks from the park when we ran out of road. A river barred our path, so I cranked the wheel hard to draw the sniffling horde around with us.

"Cut over about a block so the buildings give us some cover." Alex pointed.

I did, and the zombies followed. Unfortunately, our cover didn't last. The message had gotten out. We were headed back, and the human tide began to turn our way. They were crossing over from the adjacent street, and if we didn't hurry, they'd cut us off before we had a chance to get back.

"Crap, here they come."

Snot Zombies poured into the road from the adjacent block, but I floored the accelerator enough to get ahead of them. They were close behind, making our margin for error about as thick as a duck's feather. If Simeon had any idea we were going for something other than the fountains, we'd be done for.

"You better jump into my pack, Quack." I shot him a quick glance. "No time for you to get airborne.

I leaned forward and he followed my instructions, wriggling in as best he could as Trafalgar Square came into view.

As expected, Simeon stood sentinel between a pair of zombie-filled fountains. The pillar, touted as the world's smallest police station, remained unmolested and closer to us. I waited until the very last moment to avoid tipping our hand, then cranked the wheel.

The car lurched to the right in a tight swerve of screeching tires and brakes. We jerked the door handles and jumped out just before the trailing Snot Zombies caught up. Simeon realized his mistake and heeled his mount into a run. Too late. Alex jerked the door open to the police box and the Envisage Splice took us away in a vomit inducing swirl of light and sound.

CHAPTER TWELVE

I staggered off the huge Envisage Splice elevator into the marble lobby of the Judas Agency and promptly yarffed into the polished brass trashcan strategically placed at the opposite corner.

"Unbelievable." I heard a thump and turned my head enough to see Alex pound the wall next to me with the side of her fist.

"I'm having a moment here." I moaned. "Can you give me a little room?"

Alex looked down as if she had just noticed me, then scoffed. "Finish up. It's not like you're the first."

She motioned to a little pedestal next to the trashcan where a box of tissues stood. I straightened, pulled a few out and cleaned myself up, then stepped to the left to separate myself from the scene of the crime.

"Better?" Alex crossed her arms.

"When you say this has happened before, did you mean to me or to you?"

"I can't believe Simeon has … done … how could he …" Alex hit the wall again, this time much harder, completely ignoring my question. Then she hit it again and again.

"I think she's having a breakdown," Quack said in my head. He peeked out over my shoulder from the backpack. "I used to see this in the park before you ducknapped me. Lots of drinking, then one human goes rogue and there's lots of crying. Usually, someone throws up afterward though, not before."

"Get out of sight, Quack." I chided in my mind. "The last thing we need is for you to be spotted by another agent around here."

"Fine. I was just trying to help. Try patting her head. That always seems to work."

I felt Quack wriggle into the pack and I glanced around the area to be sure no one saw him. Thankfully the Envisage Splice launch area resided in an isolated area of the agency, for obvious reasons, so there weren't many people wandering around.

"Woah." I reached out and put a hand on Alex's shoulder then remembered Quack's advice about staying out of punching range. A jolt of panic almost made me pull away, but I held my ground. Alex stopped hitting the wall, and for a second, I wondered if I may have made a mistake, but then her muscles relaxed, and she turned to face me.

"I'm sorry about taking us up there. I had no idea Simeon had grown so powerful. I can't believe I let him ..." She trailed off and I expected her to face the wall in frustration again, but she let out a breath instead. "That guy is something of a personal thorn in my side. I know you don't remember, but you and I did a lot to put him in that saddle, unknowingly of course. We always planned to tear him down, but now ... I think we may have waited too long. It's too late. And poor Ryan."

I nodded, feeling frustrated that she was telling me about memories I didn't have and wishing I could share them with her. I could see her pain and frustration and felt I should be ... deserved to be, punishing myself alongside her, but had no recollection as to why.

"I'm sorry." A lame response, but it was all I could think of.

"Listen, I know I can't remember much of what we did together, but maybe I have an outside perspective here."

She looked at me, raising an eyebrow but didn't say anything.

"I'm just tossing this out there, Mr. Clueless." Quack broke in. "I may not be able to see what's going on, but when she pauses without saying anything it means proceed with an extreme lack of stupid comments."

Alex's eyebrow remained aloft, and she nodded, reminding me she could also hear Quack's intercranial commentary.

I sighed.

"All I'm saying is these things are powerful. Crazy biblical power, like Sammy said."

"Sammy is not part of your smart vocabulary." Quack whispered, trying to help.

I ignored him.

"I can tell you don't like Sammy. Maybe I don't either, I don't remember, but maybe she has a point. Maybe this is too big for us. If these Horsemen are out to do their thing, maybe our only course of action is to let it take its course and pick up the pieces afterward."

Alex's expression darkened and I knew my words had fallen on deaf ears.

"So, you want to let all the people you saw Topside die."

"I think they're pretty much dead already, but —"

"They're not dead." She poked a finger into my chest. "They're alive and trapped in a hell all their own, but they will be dead if we can't help them. So will Ryan, who is trapped in that body with Simeon, and so will the millions of people who are killing one another in the Unites States right now thanks to War."

I remained unconvinced, and Alex could see it written all over my face. I felt for all those people, I did, but sometimes you had to choose the smart battle. Alex was thinking with her heart instead of her head.

"Let me tell you a story." Alex looked at me, losing a bit of the anger behind those hazel eyes. "There was this guy. He was a good guy, but he threw in with a bad group of people. Family business. Happens to a lot of us. That family hurt people, destroyed lives, victimized human beings and tore apart entire families. Mothers, fathers and children too. This guy knew it but chose to stand back because he didn't think he could fight. He busied himself doing other things for the business that didn't involve hurting the people directly, but he still helped to make the business a success, so inadvertently he did just as much damage even though he told himself he was keeping his hands clean."

"I hear what you're saying but —"

Alex put up a hand.

"I'm not done. In the end this guy had to face what he had done. Finally had to see all the horrible things he was responsible for even though he had hung back. His hands were just as dirty. He fought and he won ... and he lost, but he stopped his family from hurting those people ever again. For him it was worth it, but he also has to live with the consequences of his actions, or inactions for the rest of eternity. The guilt of thousands of lives will hang on him forever."

Alex let her words sink in. I held little doubt as to the identity of this mysterious guy. In that moment, part of me was glad I didn't have my memories, but I couldn't help but wonder how painful the shadowed details of that story would be when they returned.

"Millions of people are going to die if we can't find a way to stop this." She put her hands on my arms, looking at me with pleading eyes. "Gabe, you and I are it. I'm drawing a line in the sand. Imagine the guilt you will carry if you don't draw that line with me, whatever the cost."

I nodded. "You're right."

"I know." She grinned and pulled me into a hug.

I hugged her back, enjoying having her close. "And Sammy's an idiot."

"Now you're using the smart words," Quack said. "You can use Sammy as long as idiot is in the same sentence."

We both chuckled as we let go.

"So, what do we do next?" I asked. "Not to belabor the point, but the Horsemen are too powerful to stand toe to toe with. That is unless The Judas Agency has some sort of super-secret arsenal."

Alex shook her head. "No arsenal like that."

"What about more of an awareness campaign. You said The Judas Agency has all kinds of media power, right? What if we exposed them to the world and helped humanity fight for themselves?"

Alex shook her head and leaned against the wall.

"The world knows what's going on, they just don't want to see it. They've been staring War in the face for weeks and have seen Simeon working his plan for longer than that. They would rather rationalize them away through mundane explanations: smallpox outbreaks, quarantines or gang violence that escalate out of control. War could march down Wall Street in full view, and people would wave her off as nothing more than a crazy cosplay character."

"A cosmic what?"

She rolled her eyes. "No. It's dressing as … don't worry about it. Right now we need to focus on this maddening situation. By the time society wakes up to realize what's really happening, it will be too late. Reality is harsh. Reality on the level of The Nine and the Judas Agency is too much for humanity's tiny mind to process."

"So what then?" I shrugged. "I'll help however I can, but I'm not going to punch a dragon in the face and tell him to eat me."

"Maybe not a dragon. I think we might have one more punch to throw."

Alex opened her mouth to say more but froze as her eyes flicked to the side, noticing a newcomer wandering into the foyer.

At first, I thought Alex would just close her mouth, nod courteously, and wait for them to pass by, but as long seconds rolled on, she held her awkward position, losing all color in her face as the person approached.

"Hello, Mr. Gantry, Ms. Neveu." He smiled at Alex. "I hope I am not interrupting. I am not sure we have actually met." He reached out his hand. "I am Judas Iscariot."

CHAPTER THIRTEEN

"Oh crap." Quack shouted into my mind. "Tell me if you're about to die again. I can't dodge anything from inside this stupid backpack. Don't get shot … or stabbed with anything long enough to go all the way through you. Like a sword. Is he carrying a sword?"

"Calm down." I thought at him. "He just wants to shake hands."

I reached out to return the impeccably dressed man's greeting. He wore a black-on-black silk suit with unkempt hair and beard that somehow maintained the perfect balance between style and carefree leisure. Even though he smiled, I could see the severe man behind the facade. Nonetheless, he seemed affable and charming enough to me. Alex clearly felt otherwise.

"Nice to meet you, sir." I offered him my warmest smile. "Not often you meet the legend behind the green curtain."

Judas let go of my hand and looked a little perplexed.

"The Wizard of Oz. I guess you don't watch much television down here. It's an old movie."

I looked at Alex who stood frozen next to me. She had at least managed to coax her mouth shut, but she looked so stiff I was beginning to wonder if we would have to wheel her away on a stretcher.

"This is my partner, Alex."

I nudged her arm and she staggered a little.

"Sorry," she finally said then offered a hand in greeting.

Judas took it, but kept his eyes on me, making me feel a little like a parakeet in a pet store. "So, what are you doing here? Returning from a mission?"

"Yeah," I said holding his gaze. "We're just coming back from a little recon in Europe."

He nodded. "I heard something about that. A possible plague sweeping the continent. Your work?"

He looked from Alex, then to me in question.

"Not exactly." Alex stammered. "More of a research and maintenance mission."

"I see." Judas clasped his hands behind his back and began to circle our position. Eyeing us up and down. "Too bad. Something like that is a true testament to the power of my agency. I would have liked to congratulate the agents responsible."

"Who wouldn't want to congratulate someone like that," I said, trying to hide my sardonic tone. "Then again, does someone capable of killing millions need that kind of recognition? They might want to remain anonymous, like Typhoid Mary or the guy who invented McDonald's."

Judas stopped pacing and Alex stopped breathing.

"He has a sword doesn't he." Quack whimpered. "I'm about to be a duck shish kabob."

"What he means to say, sir," Alex interjected. "Is that as an agent, working here is thanks enough. You provide amazing opportunities, and we intend to make the most of them."

Nice, I thought. Much smoother than my McDonald's story.

"Indeed." Judas resumed his pacing and showed Alex a gleaming white smile. "I hope the opportunities here bear many fruits for you and your partner."

Judas came full circle and halted in front of us without a word, pegging the awkward meter out at a twelve.

"Well, we should probably be going," I said, finally breaking the silence between us. "Fields to salt and people to kill, you understand."

Judas leaned in, breaching my personal space and making things even more uncomfortable. I leaned away a bit in response.

He studied my eyes for a moment then shook his head.

"Truly infuriating," he whispered to himself without losing his smile, then he stood straight as if nothing had happened.

"It was nice to have met you both. I will leave you to your missions. Remember, safety slows success."

He turned on his heel and headed back the way he came. I raised an arm ready to question his strange comment, but Alex caught it in one hand and covered my mouth with the other.

"Thank you, sir. We won't let you down."

We stood for several seconds watching his exit, then Alex let go and padded after to be sure he had left. When she returned, her face was a taut mix of panic and anger.

"What was that?'

I shrugged my innocence at her. "What? I thought I was being nice."

"Who wouldn't want to congratulate the killer of millions … or the guy who invented McDonald's?"

"Do you have any idea how many people die of heart disease every year?"

Alex punched me in the arm. "That was Judas Iscariot. Like, *the* Judas Iscariot. If he has any idea of what we're doing, the Gnashing Fields will seem like a summer vacation. I've heard horror stories that would make your toes curl."

For some reason Llamas popped into my mind but I dismissed it. What would a supervillain do with a Llama?

"Do you think he heard anything?" Alex cast a glance down

the hall as if she thought Judas might reappear around the corner.

"Naw," I said, lowering my voice anyway. "But let's move on to the next part of your plan. If he's off to alert the Gestapo, I'd rather be gone before they get here."

Alex nodded. "You up for another trip in your favorite rocket ship?"

I glanced at the Envisage Splice elevator and moaned. "If we have to, but please tell me we aren't walking out of the frying pan and into the volcano again."

Alex shook her head. "Not this time. This guy isn't even on the radar yet."

"Who is he?"

"Let's just say this is going to be a day to re-acquaint you with old friends. This guy really is the less hostile type, at least he was the last time we saw him."

"Okay, but if we're going Topside, I want a burger and fries. Suicide is way more palatable when it's drenched in partially hydrogenated oil."

CHAPTER FOURTEEN

Alex pulled on my arm as I schlucked a rain boot out of a six-inch mud pit in the middle of a lush, grassy field.

"And you told me you didn't want to wear those things." Alex grinned as I yanked my second boot out of the same muddy vacuum and stepped up to the small dry access road.

"There is no way you could have known I would end up in the only mud pit for as far as the eye could see."

Alex laughed. "I could have drawn a circle around it and colored it red, I was so sure you would land in something like this. Why do you think I forced you to wear those ridiculous yellow boots? They're the only thing saving you from the rain-soaked napalm that would have melted your legs off when you landed."

I let out a little shiver thinking about what would have happened if I had worn my regular boots. I didn't have any direct memories of coming into contact with rainwater, or rainwater-soaked mud, but Alex made her descriptions sufficiently graphic to deter me from trying.

"It'll be nice to get my memories back so I can stop all these terrible landings. I'm sure I got pretty good at them. Right?" I grinned.

"Sure you did. A real pro." She snarked. "Don't touch the gooey brown stuff on your shoes, okay?"

I wilted. "Do I get anything right? I'm beginning to think I just screw things up and make your life difficult."

Alex actually snorted at that.

"I think you pretty much defined the basis of our entire relationship."

Quack popped his head out of my backpack and looked around.

"Where are we now? Smells like water but I don't see any. Seems like sort of a tease."

"We're in East Asia."

"Asia?"

I peered around at the massive expanse of tall grassy lands. Save a ramshackle building here and there I saw no hint of civilization. Wind blew the fields in emerald waves as the horizon kissed the landscape with its deep blue sky. I inhaled the smell of grass and clean air. It was one of the most beautiful and peaceful places I could imagine. Too bad I had a feeling we were there to screw it all up.

"I thought Asia was all cities and people. Hong Kong, Shanghai, Tokyo."

Alex shook her head. "You should really start using the agency's computers."

"What's a computer?" I blinked at her with no small amount of ignorance.

"Remember that thing about making her life difficult?" Quack said. "Listen more, talk less."

"Fine. I'm sorry I don't know everything. I'm sorry I have amnesia. I'm just trying to get some perspective. Tell me about how Asia has no people." I crossed my arms and squinted out at the soft rippling fields.

"You're cute when you're pouty, but stop it." Alex chuckled. "Yes, there are lots of cities, but I looked it up. Asia produces and consumes ninety percent of the world's rice, not to mention almost half the world's sugarcane and other produce. These rice fields represent seventy-five percent of Asia's caloric intake. Can you imagine what would happen to the billions of people who depend on this food source if it were suddenly gone?"

I stared at the picturesque landscape seeing it with a whole new appreciation.

"Let me guess. I bet it is just about harvest time."

Alex gave me a little shove.

"Look at you being all smart without a computer. A few weeks ago, these fields would have been flooded. Pretty much a nightmare scenario for you and me, but they are all drained and ready to go, ripe for the picking ... which is why we're here."

"You think Famine is in the area."

Alex nodded.

"I found this article about a rise in insect infestations and locusts that seems to be harassing this region. The swarm is getting big, but with all the other insanity War and Simeon are spinning up in the world, it hasn't hit national news."

"You think someone is controlling the bugs." It was a statement, not a question.

"Who do we know that has that very same power and refuses to return to The Nine?"

I blinked.

"Am I supposed to guess? Bugsy Malone, no wait, Bugs Bunny. Jiminy Cricket feels a little too spot on."

Quack snorted a laugh in my head. "I have no idea who you're talking about, but I love the way you try to get her to punch you all the time."

Alex pulled up short of jabbing me in the shoulder then put her arm down.

"Fine, Mr. Comedian. I'm sorry I forgot for a second that you wouldn't remember."

She took a breath to continue, but a shout caught both our attention and the three of us turned in unison to see where it had come from.

A man, small in stature, wearing a straw hat sprinted up the road straight for us. We watched him come, rambling and shouting the whole way. I didn't understand a word coming out of his mouth as it was all in Chinese.

He stopped for only a moment grasping the sleeve of my jacket trying to drag us along with him. When we didn't go, he kept running, still shouting his warning to anyone who may be ahead of him.

"Well, that seemed foreboding," Quack said, as we all turned to see more people coming over the horizon.

"How big did you say that swarm is?" I asked.

"I'm not really sure. I know it's growing and that we should be just ahead of it. I figured this would be the best place to spot ...you know."

"The friendly neighborhood locust-man?"

"Something like that."

Quack popped himself the rest of the way out of the backpack and stretched his wings so he could glide down to the ground.

"I don't know about you two, but this plague sounds pretty good to me. I've been starving all day. Bring on the bugs. My stomach has never met a swarm it couldn't match."

I glanced down at Quack in disbelief. "You have faced a swarm of locust before?"

"Don't harsh my vibe. You know what I mean."

Farmers speed by us on foot, and we had to step off the road to allow two trucks full of people to amble by. Silence gave way to shouts of panic, groaning motors and tires on gravel. Scooters, motorcycles and even horses brought billows of dust from the dirt road. As they passed, the cloud settled leaving one last equine to lope toward us on the path.

The moment I laid eyes on him I knew this was our rider.

Clad in black, he wore a weather-beaten shawled top that flapped against the breeze, canvas pants and a worn-out black pair of Converse All Stars. The only exception to his dark garb was the grass-colored sedge hat tied under his chin with a black ribbon. He slumped in his saddle, face downturned and obscured by his hat as if weary from long travels, but his mount showed no such fatigue.

The stallion was black as night with a flowing mane and familiar wild eyes. The majestic animal scanned the land, ears flicking this way and that, ever alert for danger, but his gait was steady and sure, drawing him ever closer to where we stood,

"Should we be getting ready to fight or something?" I clenched my fists, suddenly feeling very naked and exposed on the open abandoned road.

"I don't think so, but watch for my signal just in case."

"Signal?" I shout-whispered as the horseman drew close. "What signal?"

"Jake?" Alex held up her hand to shade her eyes as the horseman pulled up alongside us. "I sure hope that's you."

CHAPTER FIFTEEN

When he turned his eyes to peer at us, I flinched in anticipation only to find a typical twenty-something longhaired stoner hiding underneath.

"What are you two doing here?" His voice full of genuine mirth and joy. "You're a little far from your usual territory. Just so you know, there isn't a decent bathroom for miles."

Alex laughed. "Tell me about it. You look good. Real good. What are you up to?"

"I don't get it," Quack said. "I thought this was supposed to be one of the bad guys."

I shrugged and kept my eyes on them, feeling equally as perplexed by the exchange. "Alex said they ... we, were friends. Maybe she was serious."

"Well, I don't like it. Sleeping with the enemy and all that. One second your buddy-buddy, the next, some fat bird is trying to shove you out of the nest before you even have feathers."

I couldn't help but turn my eyes down to him brooding quietly on the ground next to me.

"Sorry. Traumatic childhood. Don't get chummy. That's all I'm saying."

I nodded and turned my attention back to the conversation at hand.

"Big question is, what are you doing way out here on this beautiful landscape? Seems like a long way from home for you too."

For someone who was supposed to be one of the most powerful and fearsome forces ever witnessed on the planet, he became more than a little sheepish.

"That's sort of a long story," he said. "You remember last time we met I wasn't in the best of health?"

Alex nodded.

"Well, I ran into this nice lady who gave me this."

Jake pulled a necklace out from under his linen top cover and held it out for us to see. It was an artful representation of weights and scales all done up in gold.

"Very nice. What does it do?"

"I was a little skeptical at first, but she said it would not only cure me, but make it so I never had to go back to The Nine again. By then I wasn't sure which part would fall off my body next, so I was in no position to argue. I would have tried anything. Nothing happened right away, and I almost threw the thing out, but the next morning I woke up good as new."

"This horse showed up with the bargain?" Alex reached out to touch its nose, but it flinched away. Not so much in fear but in warning.

Jake slumped a little and took on that sheepish look again.

"I know you're here to talk me out of this, but I did a lot of thinking. I really did. Why shouldn't I look out for myself? You're down there doing the same thing at the Judas Agency. We all were. I work for a different organization now, that's all."

"Jake, this is not the same and you know it. What we do at the Judas Agency, it's bad, even global, but this means the end ... of everything. You must see that."

Jake's gaze fell to the ground, and he didn't say anything for a minute then he reached up and thumbed his talisman.

"You don't understand. This thing. This mantle I wear, it commands me. It gives me focus and reason like nothing ever has. It's all things, and I am its instrument. Together we fulfill a greater purpose."

Jakes eyes went glassy, and I reached out to pull Alex back a couple of paces. Jake didn't seem to notice. His gaze was now on the horizon.

"I will see this through, and nothing will stand against us. Nothing *can* stand against the will of the Horsemen. I am Famine. I sweep the land of sustenance and leave but barren ground. Life shall wither in my wake and the world will burn."

Jake, or rather Famine, heeled his horse, and they raced away, trailing a cloud of dust and laughter.

"I don't think you should be allowed to choose your own friends anymore." Quack looked up at Alex, ruffled his feathers and smoothed them down again.

The silence that followed lasted only a few seconds before we heard the hissing wings of calamity on the wind. We all turned to see what was to come. If Quack wanted to eat his way out of this one, he might want to call a few friends of his own.

CHAPTER SIXTEEN

"Get behind me." Alex turned to face the oncoming swarm of insects as if it were nothing more than a spring shower. I stood behind her with considerably more trepidation.

The cloud crested the horizon, slowly at first. More dark distortions than any desirable mass. Then the real swarm came. Black, swirling and terrible. It reached as far as the eye could see, blotting out the entire skyline like a living fog.

"I don't know what kind of bug spray you have in your pocket, but you don't have enough." I put a hand on Alex's shoulder to pull her away, but she shrugged me off.

"Not this time," she said. "This time we stand and fight."

"Excuse me." Quack reached out and pecked at Alex's boot with his bill to get her attention. "I think I'm with the memory infant on this one. I'm a duck. I'm not about to be a smorgasbord for my own buffet. Those things will eat us alive"

"They are locusts." Alex set her feet. "They don't eat people ... or ducks. We're staying."

I watched as the swarm grew and grew, advancing on us like vile despair. The buzzing was tireless and unending, pounding at the air, the ground, and my mind. It was so pervasive I felt the vibration on my skin.

"Call me crazy, but I'm betting that welcome party is all inclusive. Locusts might be the guests of honor, but I guarantee there are other gate crashers too." I gestured up the road to where we touched down at our splice point. "Maybe we should get a little closer in case—"

"No!" Alex shouted, part to be heard over the noise and part in anger. "We are staying. I could not bring myself to hurt the people in London, but these are a bunch of bugs. We can do something about these."

I felt a tug at my pant leg and looked down to see Quack plucking at the material with his beak.

"Listen I am all for doing my part here, but do you mind putting be up in your backpack again. If you two are going to turn yourselves into a real-life pest bait, I would just as soon hide. I swear I'll keep my beak outside the zipper and eat as many bugs as I can."

I reached down and wrestled Quack into the open pack without an argument. At least one of us should live to tell this story. I wasn't even sure how these bugs would affect us. Alex told me we could heal from any injuries as long as we were Topside. Unless, that is, said injuries were inflicted by rainwater or another Niner's power. Jake was a Niner. Or at least he used to be and calling these bugs was apparently his power. Did that mean we were vulnerable? Quack certainly was, though he was afforded some protection in my backpack. I wondered if there was room in there for me.

"I don't mean to belabor the point here, but you aren't carrying anything to fight with."

Bugs began to whiz by our heads as the swarm got closer.

"What are you planning to do, whip off a flip-flop and start swatting? You aren't even wearing flip-flops!"

Alex held up her hands as the darkness closed on us. More

and more locusts, and as expected, about a million other insect species filled the air. Flies, gnats, roaches, mosquitoes, bees, wasps and every other kind of flying bug buffeted our bodies. Alex raised her hands against them all. I waited in expectation and wonder. Whatever it was she was about to do she needed to do it now.

With a grim shout of determination, she opened her palm and there within her hand floated a softball sized ball of flame.

I stared at it with a swirl of mixed feelings. Manifesting fire out of thin air was cool, if not mildly impressive. However, manifesting it on this scale was like standing against the Nazi Blitzkrieg with a matchstick.

"No offense." I began to fight some genuine panic and I tried not to open my mouth any more than I had to for fear a bug would fly in. "I don't think that's going to be enough to—"

"Shut up. Put your hand on my shoulder and don't let go!"

The urgency in her voice was clear, so I did as she asked without question. I could feel her tense under my touch, brace for something to happen, but nothing did.

Insects landed on me now, alighting on my legs, chest and face. I tried to stay calm but when a locust landed on my nose and began to crawl across my eye, I could no longer maintain my composure. A shriek of pure panic and emotion escaped my lips and with it something else.

The connection between Alex and I came to life. Somehow my torrent of panic and emotion suffused Alex's flickering ball into a torrent of heat and flame.

At first, the sudden inferno was more terrifying than the swarm itself. The heat and smoke hit me like a blast furnace and everything around us ignited as well. Bugs cooked off, crackled and rained down in millions of tiny cinders. I used my spare hand to swipe away the insects that still clung to my face and body, fearing the radiant heat might get to them too.

"Hang on, Gabe. Keep feeding me your energy." Alex

laughed manically as she waved her hands through the air, sweeping the torrent from side to side.

I squeezed her shoulder tighter, fearing what would happen if I let go. The range of her flames was impressive. Had I not been standing behind her my face would have melted like candle wax, but the real magic was in the chain reaction that occurred above.

The swarm was so dense that her flames jumped from insect to insect in a flash fire. The cloud glowed with the spreading conflagration, raining tiny embers down from the sky. As insane as fire falling from the sky seemed, I could not shake the feeling that I had seen this before. I wanted my memories back, but as time went on I had to wonder what sort of memories I would be getting when they did return.

"Wow." I let go of her shoulder and choked out a cough against the stench of burning bugs. The moment I let go, the inferno in her hands reduced to a small fireball again. "I guess you did have something better than a bug bazooka in your pocket. When were you going to tell me about that little trick?"

Alex extinguished the rest of the flame and turned to look at me. "I just did. You and I sort of work a symbiosis thing somehow. You figured it out not too long ago. Comes in handy every once in a while." Her smile was nothing short of infectious. "Chalk one up for the good guys. Jake might be able to bring up another swarm, but it will take him a while, and he won't be finding any bugs around here."

She coughed and waved away the smoke that grew between us.

"Excuse me, oh great and powerful insect slayers." Quack poked his head out of the zipper far enough to see how things had progressed. "I love that you're taking this time to bask in your victory, but you may want to check the battlefield."

I turned and felt my grin fall to horror. The smoke all around us may have started as the smoldering remnants of our flying foes, but in our haste to destroy them, Alex had failed to consider the very thing we were here to protect. Miles of raining embers had lit the grassy waves of rice fields aflame. Every hillside, every building, every last tree and shrub was consumed in the fiery aftermath. We had defeated the oncoming swarm only to destroy the crops more efficiently than any insect ever could have. The wildfires would only grow and destroy more fields. By the time they were under control, Jake would possess a whole new swarm ravaging the country from another direction. Alex knew it too.

She fell to her knees and put her face in her hands. "No. No-no-no-no-no-no. This can't be happening."

The sheer sadness and defeat I heard in her voice made my chest hurt. I crouched down next to her, acutely aware that we were on a dirt road in the middle of a growing wildfire.

"No matter what I do, I just make things worse," She cried. "You were right. We should have sat back and watched from the sidelines. At least I wouldn't be helping them."

I put a hand on her shoulder.

"You're doing the best you can," I said. "And that was pretty impressive. Super impressive, actually. It almost worked."

I pulled her hands away from her face, exposing tears, and wrapped my arms around her. "You were right, not me. We have to try—keep trying. I know I don't have my memories, and I am a huge pain, but I promise one thing. I will stand by you. What you're doing is right. So what if we make a mistake? At least it's something. Sooner or later, we're going to make a difference."

Alex snorted a laugh then coughed. The smoke was getting thicker, making it hard to see or breathe. Then something occurred to me.

"We're dead. Why are we coughing?"

Alex half laughed half coughed. "I'm crying, you're suffering from preconceived expectations. None of this can hurt us. Not permanently anyway. It won't feel good, but we will heal if we were burned."

"Some of us are not members of the International House of the Afterlife Club." Quack shouted into our minds. "Feel free to light yourselves on fire some other time. For now, maybe we could get the live water foul's sensitive respiratory system out of the danger area."

I winced at Alex. "We should probably go."

Alex nodded and pulled a tissue out of her coat pocket to dab at her eyes and nose as she stood. I stood with her but noticed something fall out of her pocket as she got ready to walk away.

"You dropped something."

She glanced over and then reached to pick it up with a little laugh.

"This is actually yours." She held out her hand, showing me an ancient looking coin in her palm. "When you ... died, you left this behind somehow. I never saw it before, but I wanted to save it in case it was important to you."

I looked at small piece of silver trying to recall any memories but felt nothing.

"Funny thing is now I can't get rid of it. I tried to leave the coin in my apartment for safekeeping, but I swear every time I put it down the thing ends up right back in my pocket again."

She turned her hand over to drop the coin into my hand and when she did the weight of the entire world fell into my palm.

CHAPTER SEVENTEEN

I woke choking and gasping for breath. Not because my lungs were full of smoke ... not completely. It was mostly because of a duck bill clamped down over my nose hampering my attempts to breathe.

"I told you that would work." Quack let go of my nose and flapped out of my reach before I could swat him away out of reflex. "Nothing shakes off unconsciousness like the fear of death."

I sputtered out a few more coughs and gasped in a breath full of smoke, then began to choke it out again. Then I realized ... remembered the smoke should not be a problem for me.

As I lay there, my entire world came back in a rush. Every memory, experience and feeling I had ever had in life or death hit me at once. It was like falling in love, losing every loved one, experiencing the joy of every new thing and learning to hate everything that ever hurt me all in one second. I didn't know whether to laugh, cry, scream or punch the ground, so I did them all at the same time.

Alex crouched down next to me and put her hand on my chest. "Are you ok?"

I panted and gathered myself there on the dirt then I looked up at Alex. "You touched the coin."

She let out an uncomfortable laugh.

"We're in the middle of nowhere surrounded on every side by wildfire with you screaming like a lunatic and the first thing you're worried about is your stupid coin?"

"Check your pocket."

Alex stared at me. "What are you talking about. You aren't making any sense. We need to get back to the splice point before the smoke gets too bad for Quack—"

"Just check your pocket."

The sheer urgency in my voice made her put up her palms up in surrender.

"All right, fine." She stood and shoved her hands in her pockets. "Nothing, now can we ..."

Her voice caught as she pulled her hand out of her right front pocket and produced the coin.

"But that's impossible."

I shook my head. "We have to get out of here."

"Oh, now you want to leave." Quack started waddling toward the splice point where we came in, keeping his head as close to the ground as he could to stay below the smoke. "The duck bonded to your soul is going to die and it's no big deal, but the girl pulls a quarter out of her pocket and suddenly we're in a rush."

I struggled to my feet and regretted it the moment I was upright. Dead or not, I could not help but be affected by the thick smoke when I stood. I coughed out a lungful and then stooped over again.

"What's going on Gabe?" Alex ducked down to my level and glared into my eyes. "Why does this thing keep appearing in my pocket? And why were you screaming?"

She opened her mouth to say something else, but I stopped her by planting a kiss right on her lips. The familiar feeling was like a warm shower on a cold day. Alex pulled away at first, but then we straightened, and she grabbed my head, deepening the kiss and redoubling the electricity between us. When we parted her eyes were wide and I couldn't help but smile and nod.

"I got my memories back."

"Thank God. For a second I thought I was going to have to kick your ass."

I laughed.

"Let's get Quack out of here." I glanced up to see that he was almost to the splice point. I took Alex's hand, and we managed to stay low as we followed him in quick succession.

"What are we going to do about this?"

Alex looked around one last time and I could see the regret in her eyes.

"We can't leave. All of this destruction, it's my fault."

I gripped her hand tighter, both to comfort her and to be sure she kept walking. "This is not your fault. It would have been gone either way. At least you tried to do something to stop it."

We hurried forward finally catching up to where Quack waited.

"Besides, we have an important meeting with a man about that coin. He is going to be very interested in the fact that you have it, and you're not going to believe what you've gotten your-self into."

CHAPTER EIGHTEEN

I refrained from telling Alex who it was we were going to see. I think she had her suspicions, but sheer disbelief kept her moving. Everyone knew where Judas's office was located. It was hallowed ground. A mystical place people heard about but dared not venture. When we stepped onto the elevator of the tallest building at the Agency, and I punched the penthouse button, Alex stared at me as if she thought I'd made a mistake. When the doors opened on the top floor, however, there could be no doubt. Something in the air turned your legs to Jell-O and your guts to a raspberry purée. Maybe it was the air freshener. It still happened to me no matter how many times I came here. You'd think I'd be over it by now.

"Gabe are you crazy?"

I had to pull her by the hand just to get her off the elevator and into the horror-motif lobby. All dark wood, dim lighting and fine art depicting every measure of torture, war and death. Sort of like charm but on the opposite end of the spectrum.

She yanked her hand out of mine.

"We can't go in here." Her voice was full of whisper filled panic. "I don't think you have *all* your memories yet. If you did, you'd know anyone who wants to keep their heads attached to their bodies should never go near this place."

Alex began to dig her heels in, but she was not all out planting her feet ... not yet. "I've heard horrible stories about this place. People who come here and never return ... like ever. I don't know what you're planning, but this is a terrible idea."

I grinned. "I would like to tell you none of that is true, but it would be a lie."

"Especially the part about this being a bad idea."

The receptionist watched us approach us with her usual deadpan expression. "I don't believe you and your guest have an appointment, Mr. Gantry."

She paused for effect, then said.

"I'll buzz you right in."

The tiniest of smiles touched her lips but there was nothing friendly about it. That smile, if it were there at all, was pure mischievous evil.

"Thank you, Veronica."

Alex stared at me in wonder as I referred to the woman with first name familiarity. I didn't mention that the receptionist refused to ever give me her name, so I made a game of calling her something different every time I visited the office.

"Don't mind Veronica. She comes across all Catholic school nun, but she's a pussycat underneath."

I got ready to turn and lead Alex to Judas's office, but Veronica did something I did not expect. She stood and smiled ... at Alex.

"Hello my dear, I'm Terayn. Mr. Gantry has trouble remembering my name. It is a pleasure to meet you. If there is anything I can do to make your visit more comfortable please let me know. Mr. Iscariot can be a bit intimidating but I'm sure he will like you. Be yourself and you'll be fine."

Alex nodded like a frightened zombie.

I stared at the receptionist, my mouth agape in shock.

"Trouble remembering your name? Your name is Terayn? Why wouldn't you tell me? I can't believe you ... Make your visit more comfortable?"

"I'll just buzz you in." Terayn lilted her head to the side and shot me a not so innocent smile. "You better get in there before your friend loses her nerve."

I narrowed my eyes at Terayn and leveled a finger in her direction. "You and I are going to discuss this later, young lady."

I turned and herded a bewildered looking Alex toward the ornately carved door to our left.

"Terayn," I grumbled under my breath. "How was I ever supposed to guess that?"

The door opened of its own accord, and we walked through. Judas glanced up from his desk and started to say something, but then he saw that I had Alex in tow, his face turned three shades of purple.

"Mastema, detain her."

Mastema was one of two demons almost always present in Judas's office. The other was Procel. An eight-foot albino with red eyes and long dusky horns growing out of his forehead. He played the strong silent type while Mastema went all out homicidal sex-monkey full of claws, teeth, and steroids. She was fast, unnaturally strong, scantily clad in black leather to match her wings, and before I could blink, she had leapt off her perch behind Judas and streaked across the room.

Alex didn't stand a chance. I had seen Mastema go to work firsthand. She took her job seriously and enjoyed every moment of it. Alex was an accomplished hand-to-hand fighter, and I would put her up against any human, but she hadn't so much as twitched a pinkie before Mastema snatched her out of my grasp and pinned her against the wall.

"You have overstepped your bounds, Mr. Gantry." Judas marched around his huge obsidian desk; fists clenched at his sides. "Bringing her here not only breaks your vow it requires she pay for it as well."

The door to his office slammed shut with a boom making me jump. Everything was happening too fast.

"Procel." Judas's voice boomed with anger. "These two are going to the ditches. You will take them with Mastema. They speak to no one."

He glared into my eyes with so much fury, tears threatened to fall. I had seen him angry before, but this was different. This was disappointment. This was regret on a scale even he had trouble dealing with.

"Leave now. Never speak his name again." He looked at Procel.

"Gabe?" Alex squeaked out from behind me, but I didn't respond.

Procel began to move his massive bulk in my direction. He spread his dusky wings as if to launch himself at me, but I put up a hand in protest.

"Hold on a second." I swallowed down the panic rising in my throat. "Everyone is getting worked up over nothing. If I had betrayed any secrets the coin would have done the banishing already."

Part of the deal when you joined the Denarii Division was that you could never divulge the secret of the sect to anyone. If you tried, the coin would suck you into some sort of horrible void for all eternity, thereby protecting its secrets forever.

That brought Judas's hand up to halt the Procel freight train.

I held my breath, not quite daring to relax.

"Where is it?" Judas still looked every bit as angry but there was a glimmer of doubt there too.

"That's just it," I said. "I am no longer the possessor of said coin."

Judas's glower and voice deepened. "This is not the time to

play games, Mr. Gantry. You have no idea the misery you dance upon."

I dared a glance behind me to look at Alex. Mastema still had her pinned against the wall, sniffing seductively at her face, one clawed hand wrapped around her throat.

"If you could just call off your ..." I almost said dog but thought better of it. Turned out my diplomacy button worked when threatened with unthinkable torture. "Just call Mastema off and I can produce the coin."

Judas seemed to consider this while he huffed in several angry breaths, then he flicked his eyes over my shoulder.

"Release her."

I turned around to look at them again and Mastema made a disappointed cooing noise. She didn't let Alex go right away. Instead, she pressed her cheek to hers and breathed into Alex's ear, flicking her black tongue out to taste Alex's skin, then she backed off a step, remaining at the ready in case Judas changed his mind.

"You have five seconds," Judas growled.

"Gabe, what's going on?" Her eyes reddened on the verge of tears and her hands were up ready to fight or flee, maybe both. I had never seen her so unsure or terrified.

"Show him the coin," I said, ignoring her question.

"Not until I get some answers—"

"Show him the coin now." My voice came out in a shriek. If Judas said five seconds, he meant it. That was precisely the amount of time we had before he deep-fried our bacon.

Alex keyed in on my panicked screech and reached into her pocket to produce the coin.

Judas stepped forward to examine the small silver piece in her hand.

"That's impossible." He glanced from the coin up to her eyes. "Throw it away. Throw it as far as you can. Now!"

The command in his voice was unquestionable. Alex did it

without hesitation, hurling the coin toward the furthest corner of Judas's gigantic office. I watched it sail through the air for a moment, then seemed to lose sight of it somehow. When I looked back to Alex, the coin was in her hand again. She stared at the tarnished piece of sliver, just as surprised as I was, but no one appeared as shocked as Judas.

"This is not possible. No one takes up the coin of their own accord. They are chosen ... by me."

I raised an eyebrow and looked at him. "Maybe a higher authority decided to help you out with recruiting. I can tell you, Alex is a way better agent than I am, and she has taken it upon herself to go Topside to try and stop the Horsemen singlehanded."

"Gabe, what are you doing?" Alex started to take a step but Mastema flicked out her claws, stopping her.

"What do you mean, Horsemen?" Judas's face had faded from over-ripened plum to underripe cherry. We were definitely making progress on the anger fruit scale.

"I mean there is more than just War up there now. Our friend Simeon is Pestilence and a fellow Judas Agent exile named Jake has taken up the mantle for Famine. Alex figured them both out before they had a chance to go public and she tried to face them down alone." I hesitated then added. "Well, she had me, but I was more of a hindrance than a help with no memories."

"This is problematic." Judas rubbed at his beard in a thoughtful expression.

"Gabe." Alex snapped. "Why are you doing this?"

I could hear the pain in her voice and when I glanced at her, I saw that her tears had begun to fall. It took me a moment to realize, that to her, it seemed like I was outing her to the head of the Judas Agency as a turncoat and spy.

I shook my head and held out my hands. "Alex, I'm sorry. Calm down. You don't understand."

She wiped away a tear, glaring hatred and pain at me. I couldn't stand seeing her like this.

"This isn't what you think. I—"

"Perhaps I can shed some light on the situation." Judas interrupted. "Mastema, if you please."

The demon made no such hesitation this time. With a powerful flap of her wings, she soared back to her perch behind Judas's desk. Procel seemed to have stood down too, relaxing to his usual stony stature.

"Ms. Neveu." Judas held out a hand and Alex took it, allowing Judas to lead her to one of two chairs that fronted his gigantic desk. She didn't even seem to notice that it was framed with human bone rather than wood. I sat down in the other one and kept my mouth shut, a monumental effort of will on my part, while Judas spoke.

Judas took up a position opposite Alex and leaned against his desk then appraised her thoughtfully. "It seems you and I have a great deal to talk about."

CHAPTER NINETEEN

"Normally this is the point at which I would offer you a choice."

Judas had spent the better part of two hours explaining and talking about the Denarii Division, its objectives, duties and burdens. Much longer I noted, than he talked to me. I swore my pitch was all of fifteen minutes.

"Choice? I had a choice?" I said, breaking my silence. "You all but tricked me into taking the coin."

Judas turned and stared at me with serious eyes. "No one tricked you. You accepted your appointment of your own accord."

"You threw the coin at me, and I caught it. I had no idea touching that thing meant I was in the club."

"You could have allowed the coin to fall. You chose to catch it. Besides, given a real choice, you would have waffled for weeks before coming to the same decision."

"You don't know that. I might have turned you down."

Judas pinched the bridge of his nose. "No, although it is times like these that make me wish you would have."

Alex let out a snort of laughter. "I work with this every day."

Judas turned to her looking just as serious. "Perhaps I can arrange some sort of annoyance compensation."

"I'm not sure even the Agency has that much money." She laughed.

Judas nodded. "You are probably correct."

"Hey," I said. "You two don't get to team up. I was here first."

"I don't see that you have a choice in the matter." Judas answered glancing up at me. "And I will look into that fee. You certainly earn it."

Alex laughed again.

"So, this is why you were always working against me on our missions. You were a legitimate double agent for Judas, himself. I always knew you were a goody-two-shoes."

"I worked against you because what you were doing was wrong." My voice cracked with indignation. "And don't forget you're now a coin carrying member of the two-shoes club as well."

Alex looked over at Judas. "You're right. He would have defiantly accepted."

I groaned. "I'm not sure I'm going to like this."

"I'm sure you're not going to like this." Alex smiled. "But I am going to enjoy every second."

"All joking aside, I want you to understand the significance of your position. Accepting a post as one of the thirty Denarii agents is not just an honor, it is a duty and often a terrible burden. We fill our charge no matter the personal cost or the cost to those we care about. It can be difficult and at times feel insurmountable, but we do it nonetheless and you are only the second in all of history to be *chosen* rather than selected for the position."

Alex looked confused. "What do you mean chosen?"

I was a little confused as to the distinction myself but was glad Alex asked instead of me.

"I mean usually I select candidates, invite them to my office, and they either accept the coin or ..."

He let the statement fall there, and I could not help but wonder what happened if someone decided against accepting the position.

"You took up the coin of your own free will. The coin should have never been there in the first place, but remain it did. A higher power placed the mantle before you and you took it up, initiating you into the Denarii Division."

"You said she was the second." I sat forward in my bone chair, suddenly curious. "Who was the first?"

Judas turned his gaze to me and the moment he did, I realized the answer to my question stood right in front of me.

"You," I whispered, in shock.

He nodded in affirmation. "I was the first and only one chosen until now."

Alex sat back in her chair, her eyes going wide.

"But why me? I'm nothing special."

"That's not true." I turned to face her. "You have a good heart, and you fight for what's right, even when you don't have to. You always do. You're the right man ... woman for the job if there ever was one."

"I agree with Mr. Gantry for once." Judas offered her a warm smile. "I believe you will make an excellent agent, although why you were chosen has yet to be seen. Keep your eyes and ears open. I find most answers are revealed in time."

Alex nodded, taking a bit of comfort in that.

"Hey, I hate to interrupt, but how much longer do you think this little pow-wow is going to last? It's getting stuffy in here and I want to get out."

Alex and I locked eyes in a panicked gaze. Quack was still in his backpack. I had set him on the floor then forgotten he was there.

"What is it?" Judas peered around the room. "What's wrong?"

"Perhaps it is the third member of their party?" Procel rumbled from the back of the room. "I smelled him when you walked in. I wondered when he would reveal himself."

"Third member?" Judas's complexion began to shift to the violet spectrum again as he stood trying to make sense of Procel's admission.

"Before you unleash your assassins again, I need to point out no one has been sucked into the void of the coin. I have a soul bond with this creature, and he is a part of me. I didn't mean for him to find out about all of this, but it was probably inevitable given the fact that we have to be together all the time."

I reached down to the backpack next to me and unzipped the top. Judas leaned forward looking ready to pounce on whatever came out. When Quack popped his head out, Judas jumped back in surprise.

"It's a duck."

I nodded. "Yes, it's a duck."

"You are bonded to this creature?"

I nodded again.

Judas stared at Quack for another minute then did something I had never seen him do before. He let out a genuine, honest to goodness, laugh.

"I have no doubt I will regret this question, but what on earth led you to be bonded with a duck?"

"I never wanted to bother you with the details." I shrugged. "I developed a soul leak, you know from playing with my Topside powers too much, and it turns out the only way to fix it was to bond with another living creature. We had a plan to fix it, but things went a little sideways. One thing led to another and now the duck and I are BFFs."

Judas blinked.

"BFF," I said. "Best friends forever. Come on, you have to catch up on a little pop culture."

"I assume you can communicate with the bird, or you would not be so concerned about revealing our secret."

I nodded, then cursed myself for being so stupid. I should have just said Quack couldn't talk. Why would Judas even think he could? At least all our secrets were out in the open now. I wouldn't have to lie anymore.

"The duck heard everything?" Judas said.

"Yeah, I heard. How could I not hear? The guy never stops talking."

"Yes," I said. "But he can only communicate with Alex and me so there is no one he could tell." I omitted his ability to speak with Sammy. We were in dangerous waters. I didn't want to punch holes in the boat.

Judas thought about it for a second, then sighed.

"So be it, though I regret you did not confide in me with your troubles regarding the leak. I might have been able to help you. Bonding your soul to another creature isn't the only way to fix this problem."

"What? Now you tell me."

"As I said, you didn't ask, so I was unable to help. Regarding your feathered friend knowing your secret, the coin is its own judge and jury. If it sees fit to leave you alone, then so shall I."

He leveled a finger in my direction and narrowed his eyes. "That doesn't mean I will not deal with impropriety. If I believe you are stepping outside the lines, I can and will reciprocate. If that happens, you may well wish the coin had taken you."

I gulped and noticed his threat was in no way pointed at Alex.

"Understood." It was all I could manage while Judas had a loaded finger aimed at my face.

"Good," he said. "Are there any other surprises you wish to reveal or does that about wrap up our meeting?"

I glanced over at Alex and then back to Judas again.

"Actually, we hoped you might give us some sort of guidance on what to do about the Horsemen. We want to stop them, but they're too powerful. We don't know what to do. Do you have any ideas?"

"Indeed." Judas rounded his desk to sit down. "You are to do nothing about the Horsemen. They are a neutral force and thus no power from the Heavens or Hell shall impede their advance. Any attempt on our part to intercede will only make it worse. You will stand down and let events play out as they are meant to. Besides, you will both be quite busy with your new assignments."

Alex and I looked at each other as Judas pulled out a set of forms from his desk and began writing with his raven quill.

"You will both be assigned new partners. Train with them and begin reporting back to me on your missions as soon as possible."

CHAPTER TWENTY

"Nothing?" I said.

At the same time Alex said, "New partner?"

Then we switched, reversing the words but still repeating them at the same time. "Nothing? New partner?"

Judas stopped writing and looked at the two of us. "Yes, new partners and you will do nothing about the Horsemen. I feel both parts are quite clear."

"Yeah," I said a little more like an angsty teenager. "But the why on both parts is a little hazy."

Judas laid his quill down across his papers and let out a breath as if to steady his patience. I was proud of him. On any other day he would be screaming my face off by now. Either he really liked Alex, or he was learning to control that anger button of his.

"I will begin with the need to reassign you to new partners." He folded his fingers in front of his chest and rested his arms on the desktop. "Every Denarii agent is partnered with a regular Judas agent. Typically, a successful field agent is tasked with carrying out destructive missions. It is your job to stop those missions from happening. It does no good to have two Denarii agents partnered together because one would not be preventing the other from doing anything at all. In Mr. Gantry's case that might not be much of a change, but I have high hopes for you Ms. Neveu."

Alex let out a little laugh which did nothing to help our cause.

"With everything that is going on Topside right now it may take a few days to process the paperwork, but the transfers will be enacted as soon as possible."

I sighed in concession. I didn't have much of an argument since the one thing we wanted to work on together was off limits as well.

"And why ignore the Horsemen?" Alex kept her voice even and inquisitive rather than angry and accusatory. She was way better at this than me. "I don't want to overstep my bounds, but if it is our job to prevent destructive events, this seems like the granddaddy of them all."

Judas looked over at her and smiled ... he actually smiled ... again. Now she was just showing off.

"You are right, Ms. Neveu, this is a global level event, but it comes with several caveats. When you said your friend, Jake, took up the mantle for Famine you were quite literally correct. There are, in fact, four mantles. Two hidden in Heaven and the other two hidden here in The Nine. Only if they are brought together can the apocalypse occur and thus the end of the world."

Judas sat back in his chair and tilted his head as he continued.

"They were separated by design so neither side could bring them to bear without the agreement of the other. To further prevent either side from interfering, the Horsemen were created as a purely neutral force. Neither good nor evil. Therefore, neither the forces of good nor evil can influence or prevent them from carrying out their charge. Only another neutral force can stand against them and there is no neutral force known on earth or in the Heavens that is as powerful as the Horsemen."

"So, there's no hope?" This time Alex had a harder time keeping the frustration from slipping through. "We just sit here and watch the world end?"

To my surprise Judas shook his head.

"I said all *four* of the Horsemen must come together to bring about the end of the world. Someone infiltrated the gates of Heaven and stole the mantles of War and Famine then presented them to the Council of Seven."

I cringed at the mere mention of the name. The Council of Seven are second only to the big Red S himself. They are made up of his oldest demon generals and carry out missions that make the Judas Agency look like the Boy Scouts. No one trifles with The Council and if they were involved, this was very bad indeed.

"The Council, in turn, managed to uncover one of the mantles here in The Nine. The mantles were meant for those worthy of such a terrible task. To be granted at a time when Heaven and Earth were prepared for such an end. Instead, they were offered to those desperate for power, revenge or self-preservation. Now there is no going back."

"But you said they only had three of the mantles." I leaned forward in my chair, eager to hear the answer to my next question. "What happened to the fourth?"

Judas leaned forward as well and eyed us both in turn.

"The mantle of Death is the most powerful and deadly of them all. It completes the cycle and without it they can never bring about the full destruction they seek. That is why you will do nothing. Without Death, the other three will run their course, but in the end, their power will dwindle, and they will fail."

"But all the people that will die in the meantime ..." Alex stared at Judas in shock.

"A tragic loss, but as I have explained to Gabriel many times, we must endure to preserve and protect what is truly precious."

Alex sat there speechless. I knew how she felt. Angry, sad, frustrated, helpless. I'd been there before. Judas was immovable on this point. It was what the Denarii Division had been based upon ... what he based his life on. There was no shaking him on this. We do what has to be done.

"So, Death's mantle is safe here in The Nine somewhere?"

Judas turned his eyes on me.

"It is in a place no one knows exists. From this point on you will not speak of it or act against the Horsemen. To do so would only mean more destruction. Let the last mantle lie in its grave-yard of forgotten beliefs and the world will find its own way to heal."

Alex and I snapped our heads around in a not-so-subtle fashion to stare at one another at the same time.

"Oh crap." Quack interjected. "You two know where it is, don't you?"

CHAPTER TWENTY-ONE

Judas's words had marked the proverbial X on the spot. *Let the last mantle lie in its graveyard of forgotten beliefs.* The moment he said it, I knew right where it was hidden. I couldn't unknow, and Alex knew it too.

"I wish I could hear more than your inner dialogue right now," Quack said. "No wait, I take that back. I don't want to know what you're thinking because if what I think you're thinking is what you're thinking, I'm thinking you're both crazy."

I turned to Judas, doing my best to keep my expression placid and ignore Quack's commentary.

"Something you'd like to say?" Judas worked his inquisitor's stare back and forth between the two of us. Every time he looked at me it felt like a punch in the chest.

I shook my head. "So, the Death thingy is out."

"Mantle," Judas bellowed.

"Right, Death *mantle*." I annunciated the last word to be extra annoying. "Could we do something else, to say, indirectly assist Topside? Something like the Red Cross, only from The Nine. The upside-down Red Cross?"

That one drew a sharp glare from Judas, but I ignored it and went on.

"We could render aid without confronting the Horsemen. Maybe try to get people out of the way or—"

"You aren't getting it." Judas pinched the bridge of his nose and sucked in a deep breath. "If you save one hundred souls you will unwittingly trigger an explosion that will kill a thousand. If you help a town, something will occur to level a city. These are events beyond your comprehension or control. Nothing good or evil can intervene without massive repercussions and there is no neutral power strong enough to stand against them. Even if there were, removing a Horsemen's mantle, once it has been accepted, is impossible. I'm not just forbidding you to intervene. Intervening is not conceivable or advisable in any way. If it were, I would be the first to send you both to your deaths."

That was enough to set me back a breath or two.

"Um, thank you?"

"I can see you both share an irritating stubborn streak that I am not going to appreciate." Judas began to raise his voice in a fashion I liked to refer to as the Evil Knievel ramp to rage.

"As of this moment you are no longer partners. You are not to work together on any assignments, Agency sanctioned or otherwise. You will remain in The Nine until you are assigned to your new partners and under no circumstances will you involve yourselves in the events directly or indirectly connected to the Horsemen."

His voice had risen to a shouting spitting tirade that had Alex hugging her knees to her chest and me leaning so far back in my chair I was about to fall over.

"Sheesh," Quack said, retreating into his backpack. "I've heard bears make less noise than him."

"Is there anything within my instructions and orders you find to be unclear?"

Alex shook her head in an emphatic no, but I raised a tentative finger into the air.

"What if Alex and I worked together on an assignment unrelated to the Horse—"

"Procel, please show my two guests to the door."

Despite cutting me off mid-sentence I could not help but notice he had sicced Procel on us rather than Mastema. That was a sure sign that he felt less homicidal than usual.

I clamped my lips shut as the huge demon began to move. It was like watching a granite mountain animate to life and become a force of nature. His grey robes swayed into motion and his dusky wings swished along the floor as if too lazy or disinterested to move. His eyes, however, were living flame and cast heat upon all who dared meet his gaze.

He didn't say anything. He didn't have to. Procel just raised an arm toward the door. Alex and I were out of our chairs and moving before he could do anything else.

I swept up my backpack and took care not to jostle Quack too much as I donned the straps and secured him for our exit.

"Oh, Gabe."

I turned to see Judas retrieving something from a small ornate box on his desk.

"You may be needing this."

He flipped the item toward me and I snatched it out of the air before it could hit the ground. When I opened my palm, I held a silver Denarius. One to replace Alex's marker. I could not help but recognize the irony in the fact that he had tossed it to me a second time ... and I had caught it.

"You will receive your new Envisage Splice access pin along with your new partner. Welcome back to the agency."

"Thank you, sir."

Procel shifted in our direction, and I got ready to leave, but then I hesitated.

"I don't suppose ..."

Judas stared at me in question.

"I was just thinking, Quack is technically a member since he knows so much. Maybe he should get a coin too—"

"Mastema ..."

It was all I heard before I grabbed Alex's hand and sprinted out the door.

CHAPTER TWENTY-TWO

"Wow." Quack said from within the confines of his backpack. "That guy was a real ray of sunshine. What's his deal anyway?"

We stepped off the elevator and into the wide hall of the Judas Agency main floor. It was abuzz with agents rushing this way and that, their footsteps and voices echoing off the marbled tile and oversized ceiling. If I didn't know better, I would think we were in an innocuous building full of innocent office workers.

"Judas is known as the Great Betrayer." Alex spoke just loud enough for me to hear even though Quack would be able to hear her thoughts. "He betrayed the son of God himself for thirty pieces of silver."

"Actually." I could not help but amend. "He was chosen, or one could argue he was the only one trusted enough to carry out the horrible task required for the son of God to fulfill His destiny. He had a job to do, and he did it, no matter the personal cost."

The words resonated with me, and I could not help but hope I would be strong enough to do the same if I was ever faced with the same sort of choice.

Alex peered up at me with wide surprised eyes. "I had never thought about it that way before."

I shrugged. "Sort of what our little club is based on. Trust me, you don't want that speech from the horse's mouth. It comes with a lot more yelling and spitting."

Alex led me through the busy hall and out the front doors to the huge courtyard outside. "I believe you."

Our circumstances weighed on us as we wandered silently along a path that led us away from the busier parts of the common area. There was a large statue in the middle, an ironic depiction of Judas's betraying kiss. I wondered if Alex saw it in a different light now as well. *A job that had to be done.* Judas's part to save humanity and his reward was to spend eternity here, known for all time as the Great Betrayer.

When we got to the statue, we were far enough out of earshot to avoid being overheard and Alex jumped at the chance to speak.

"What are we going to do?" She turned to look up at me, choking out the words as she fought back tears in her eyes. "I can't believe we have to stand by and watch everything happen Topside. And losing you as a partner ... I feel like my whole world is being ripped out from underneath me."

I reached out and pulled her into my arms. She stiffened at first then relaxed and leaned into me.

"I know what you mean, believe me."

I held her for several moments, then let her go, stepping back so I could peer into her eyes.

"Hey." I wiped the tears from her cheeks. "Whatever happens, I'm always here for you."

"I know." She let out a big breath. "And I'm here for you. I mean someone has to keep you from killing yourself all the time."

"That's true." I laughed.

I leaned down to kiss her, and she kissed me back; something tender and bittersweet.

"Thank you," she said as she stepped away from me again.

"For what?" I smiled.

"For being such a stubborn do-gooder and for being my partner, even if it's only for a few more days."

"About that." I let my arms fall to my sides and I leaned against the statue behind me. "I feel like our partnership deserves to go out with a real bang."

"Oh, no." Quack rustled around in his pack. "I kept my mouth shut while you two played kissy face, but this it too much. Every time you come up with a plan, we have to dodge biker gangs, bullets and big bitches in bangin' armor. Alliteration is fun, but I am tired of trying to commit suicide."

Alex laughed.

"Quack is right, especially the bitch part. There is no path we can take that doesn't lead to ruin."

"There is one path." I raised my eyebrow at her.

She stared at me for a second in confusion then stepped back in horror.

"No. Absolutely not. That's not an option, Gabe. I'm all for coloring outside the lines but that isn't even in the same coloring book."

I took a step toward her and lowered my voice, letting my eyes dart all around to be sure no one listened in.

"Judas said there is no neutral force powerful enough to stand against a Horseman ... unless it is another Horseman. And he said Death is the most powerful of them all."

"Are you forgetting that the mantle turns you? You won't be Gabe acting like Death, you will become Death. You will bring about the apocalypse."

I shook my head in defiance. "I'll resist it. Jake and Simeon were both themselves. I think I can keep my head and fight. If something happens you can show up and slap the mantle out of me."

She shot me an evil grin. "Promise?"

"Absolutely."

She thought about it for a moment then shook her head. "What am I saying? No. This is crazy. There has to be another way."

I shrugged. "If you have an idea, I'm happy to hear it. You saw what happened every time we tried to go against them. The one time we managed to strike a blow, it turned against us just like Judas said it would. I bet those wildfires are still burning up there."

Alex looked away and I felt bad for taking that shot at her.

"I'm sorry I didn't mean that the way it sounded. I meant to say—"

"I know what you meant," she snapped, then took a breath and closed her eyes.

"Judas said we can't separate the Horsemen from their mantles. How do you plan to do that?"

"Judas says a lot of things. I find if you look at his orders as more of a challenge it makes life ... death more interesting."

"I'm surprised you haven't died way more often than you have."

I chuckled. "That makes two of us. So, are you in?"

"I can't believe I'm saying this. Yes, I'm in, but if you even begin to lose yourself, I'll slap you so hard Quack will feel it in his beak."

"Woah, leave my beak out of this."

Quack's voice made me wonder what would happen to him when I took up the mantle. Would he turn into a death duck? It was something I did not want to consider.

"Let's get going," I said. "Every second we waste, more people die. If I'm going to become Death, I want to do it before I lose my nerve."

CHAPTER TWENTY-THREE

"I think it was down here," I whispered as we crept past dusty shelves full of priceless historical objects. No one else was here, but a place like this just seemed to require hushed voices and silent footsteps. Shadowy corners, secret locations, ancient artifacts full of potential power. It was an Indiana Jones wet dream. Too bad we were in Hell instead of an exotic location full of natural wonders ... and headhunters with blowguns.

"I still can't believe all this stuff hidden in here," Alex whispered back at me.

The area wasn't huge; about the size of a small warehouse, but the shelves were packed ceiling to floor with artifacts. The rows each spanned the entire length of the space making it both difficult and overwhelming to search twenty some yards of priceless space at a time.

"Look at this. Here's the Spear of Destiny, the lance that pierced Jesus's ribs on the cross. It is supposed to hold the power to control the world. I heard Hitler even tried to get his hands on this for a while."

"I don't know who this Hitler guy is, but this place smells like moldy mothballs and wet shoe leather." Quack had his head over my shoulder appraising the area as well. "I thought we were sneaking into some sort of vault, not your grandmother's basement."

"This is a vault ... sort of, and be thankful that spear is here instead of up there where Hitler could get at it. If it grants the power to control the world, we would all be blond-haired blue-eyed Germans."

"That's ridiculous. You can't just erase everyone who doesn't have the right color plumage."

Alex and I were quiet for a moment.

"Wait, what did this Hitler guy do?"

"It was a dark time in history, my friend," I whispered back to him out loud. "It's a little too much to explain right now, but I'll tell you the story later. Just know he was not a nice guy. Sort of like the way the bubonic plague is not a nice disease."

"Woah." Quack exclaimed. "That sounds serious. What's the bubonic plague?"

Alex snorted out a laugh.

"Never mind. I'll tell you about both of them some other time. Right now, we need to stay focused."

Quack seemed content to put off his queries, but my eyes continued to wander. I saw *The Book of Toth*. A spell book that gives the user the ability to commune not only with animals but also with God. The Seal of Solomon, a ring that can imprison demons. I could definitely use that. The list went on and on. I didn't even recognize most of the objects. I would be thrilled just to sit in here and learn about the history of every item in the inventory, but at the moment I was only interested in one.

"I saw the sickle at the end of this aisle last time we were here." I gestured ahead as I looked at Alex to be sure she was still on my heels. She nodded then her eyes flicked toward something in front of us and all the blood drained out of her face. She stopped and straightened, reaching out to stop me as well. When

I turned around to see what had her so spooked, I saw why she had pulled up short.

"Oh crap."

Quack had summed up my sentiments exactly.

There, at the end of the aisle, stood an individual more frightening than any demon or monster. It was Judas Iscariot, and he had left his, *happy to see you face* at home.

He gripped an ancient looking gladius, one hand on the sheath and the other on the hilt. When he drew it out, he held the wicked weapon point down but at the ready. The blade seemed to drip with some sort of black oily power I did not want to know about. I had a feeling if any of us were to be cut with that sword, bleeding would be the last thing we'd have to worry about.

"I don't know how you found this place, but you have wandered into my personal domain. This place is sacred." His eyes showed no hint of sadness or remorse. Only rage and betrayal. "You have encroached upon the wrong territory. This is one secret neither of you will ever be allowed to divulge."

Judas stepped forward, raising his dripping gladius to a ready position. Within the confines of these shelves there was no chance to defend ourselves, not that I would want to. I was not here for a duel. I wanted to save the world and I could not do that if I were dead ... deader. Whatever.

"Stop." I held out a hand in defiance and to my surprise Judas halted his advance, if only for a moment. I was so surprised I wasn't even ready with what to say next.

"We're not here for a fight."

"I know what you're here for." Judas began to move again.

"Wait, that's not what I meant."

He paused again and I realized whatever I said next might prove to be the last words I ever uttered.

"Alex and I understand the importance of the artifacts in this room. We would never betray their secret. I would protect this place with my very soul if need be."

Alex squeezed beside me and nodded in agreement. "Gabe's right. I don't recognize everything you have in here, but I recognize enough to know what would happen if even one of these items fell into the wrong hands. We would never betray your secret. I'm sorry we intruded into you domain. It was an accident at first, and we have only been here one other time together. We would not be here now except ..."

Alex seemed to realize she had taken her explanation one sentence too far and cut it off without finishing.

Judas stood there, holding his gladius out in front of him, glaring into our eyes. Time seemed to crawl by as he decided our fate, then he grunted and lowered his weapon toward the floor. He did not put it away, but at least it was not leveled toward our chests.

"Thank you." I released the breath I didn't realize I was holding and let my shoulders fall away from my ears to a more normal position.

"Do not thank me," Judas snapped. "I may still change my mind. This place is more precious than you could possibly understand. Having so many know of its existence, much less its whereabouts, verges on the brink of absurdity."

"If I'm not overstepping my bounds," Alex prodded. "May I ask why you built this place at all? How did you come across so many artifacts?"

Judas's sword arm relaxed, and he dangled the gladius limp at his side.

"It has always been my lot in life ... and death to do what must be done. It is a difficult burden and I have never enjoyed it. At times, I would prefer an eternity deep in the Gnashing Fields to the tasks I have been called to carry out, but I would never betray the will of the Father. Here I keep a precious few of my victories. Sometimes I am called to remove artifacts from those who would use them for their own devices, whether their intentions are good or evil. That does not mean I must destroy them.

Some things are too valuable to be thoughtlessly destroyed. So here they stay. Safe from those who would exploit them. At least until now."

"Be careful, Gabe." Quack whispered into my mind. "I think he may be on to you."

"You're right." I admitted. "We ... I am here for the mantle."

Judas's sword hand twitched but I tried not to notice.

"But it *is* for all the right reasons. Death is the only force powerful enough to stop the other Horsemen. Unless we stand against them, thousands ... maybe millions will die."

Judas's eyes softened with empathy and sadness.

"You are no doubt correct," he said. "However, this is not the first time the world has endured such a horrible fate, nor will it be the last. It is my place to make the hard decision, and this is one I stand firm on. I hid the mantle of Death, and I can assure you it is now in a place in which you will never find it. The world will suffer, countless people will die, but humanity will endure."

Fury rose up from my toes, flushing my face hot and making my skin tingle with anger, but I did my best to keep my voice even.

"You're wrong this time." I took a step closer to Judas.

Judas nodded. "I will bear the consequence of that as well, if need be."

I shook my head. "Not just you."

I lifted my arm and raised a finger, pointing high overhead toward the living world above us.

"They will bear the consequences of your decision too."

I glared at Judas as he stood there, staring back at me with stone-faced implacability.

"So be it."

I opened my mouth to say more but a hand on my shoulder stayed the anger that threatened to spill out. When I turned my gaze away from Judas to look at Alex, I saw that her expression was full of sympathy and understanding. I just wasn't sure if it was for Judas or me. Maybe it was both.

"There's nothing more for us to do here." Alex patted me on the shoulder and somehow the mere touch of her hand seemed to calm me. "This is not a place for anger or fighting. It's time to go."

I paused for a moment then turned to Judas, standing steadfast and still. Somehow there was more to his expression though. In his eyes I saw sadness. Maybe even regret. In that moment I understood more about him than I ever had. He hated his job, but he did what he was called to do, no matter how hard, how costly or how devastating his actions might be. He was the wicked hand of necessity that did what had to be done. In that moment I felt for Judas. For he had been damned to a fate far worse than saving the world. He had been fated to watch it crumble ... over and over again.

We turned to leave the way we came but Judas called out to us. "Gabriel, Alex." He didn't have to say anything more. We turned to see he the gladius raised again, pointing it in our direction.

I looked him dead in the eyes, no anger or vengeance left within me. "I swear to take the secret of this place to my soul's very end. No matter our differences, none will ever learn of this place from me."

"Nor from me," Alex said.

"Me either." Quack's profession was in our head and while I appreciated it, I decided not to repeat it aloud. Better Judas forgets that there is yet a third who could reveal his secret while he held an evil dripping gladius in his hand. What did that thing do anyway? I decided I didn't want to know.

Judas lowered his weapon and nodded once, apparently satisfied by our profession.

Without a word, Alex and I turned to go, leaving Judas standing among his artifacts, miserable and alone.

CHAPTER TWENTY-FOUR

After our dismal failure at Judas's secret warehouse, there was only one place I wanted to go to drown my sorrows. Hula Harry's was the nicest place I knew in a world where the word horrible was used to describe ... well pretty much everything. I had forgotten about it the last time we were here, but I was happy my memories had brought the place back. Of course, we would be drowning our sorrows in bootleg soda, not booze. I also remembered the instantaneous and near lethal hangovers alcohol caused and I had no desire to relive that little slice of heaven.

"Hey, Dan." I raised a hand to the proprietor as we walked in. His name was not Harry, and he did not do the Hula, although I never tired of seeing his reaction when someone new asked him both questions. He eyed me with no small amount of suspicion.

"It's me," I said, as Alex and I sidled up to the bar and sat on the stools. "My brain is back to running on all three cylinders."

Dan visibly relaxed. "It's about time. I was a little worried the way you ran out of here like a scared kitten when Alex took care of those goons. You are going to have to do some serious reputation repair around here."

I shrugged. "Alex was always the scary one anyway."

"You better believe it." She winked.

"Place seems quiet tonight." I glanced around the empty bar.

He nodded by way of answer. "A firestorm swept through earlier. Some of the Woebegone were stupid enough to make a run for it and ..."

He gestured out at the room without finishing his sentence.

Firestorms were like a spring rain, only as the name implied, fire rained down instead of water, wiping out any wandering Woebegone unwise enough to be caught in the open. I was suddenly struck by the reason our Topside bug inferno had seemed so familiar, though I didn't mention it to Alex.

"I was about to close early. You two are welcome to stick around. Just lock the place up before you leave."

Alex nodded. "Thanks. Can we get a couple of drinks before you head out?"

Dan reached below the bar and produced two cans of the most valuable product in The Nine. Two ice cold Pepsi-Colas. Treats like this were a black-market commodity smuggled from Topside suppliers. Dan held a corner on that particular market thanks to a handy little trick Alex and I set up for him, and it kept his business thriving.

He popped the top on each can and slid them toward us.

"Anything for you two." He wiped his hands on the towel perpetually slung over his shoulder. "You look more down in the dumps than usual. You need to talk? I'm all ears." He raised an eyebrow as he leaned against the bar, taking on his thoughtful bartender persona.

"Thanks for the offer," I said. "But I think we just want to sit here and pout in silence."

"Suit yourself." Dan stood and made his way around the bar and headed for the door. "Don't forget to lock up the place up before you go. I don't want to come in and find a floor full of vagrants in the morning."

I laughed. "Will do, I promise."

He waved on his way out, tripping the lock on the door so no one would come in and bother us, then headed out without another word.

I don't know how long Alex and I sat there staring at the mirror behind the shelves of impotent booze. We sipped our soda, slumped over the bar and occupied the passing moments with our own thoughts. Even Quack was quiet. I assumed he was asleep in my backpack because he would have never allowed the serenity to stretch this long without filling it with his grating voice.

"This is crazy." The sudden sound of my voice was so shocking in the still silence of the bar it made Alex jump. "I can't believe we have all this power, all of these perks, and we're sitting here at Harry's while thousands of people die. There must be something we can do."

Alex readjusted herself and shot me an irritated glare for scaring her, but then she looked ahead at my reflection in the mirror and shook her head.

"I know what you mean, but what are we going to do? Judas issued some pretty specific orders, and even if we were willing to go against them, we have nothing to fight with. Anything we do to stop or hinder the Horsemen will just be turned against us."

I thought about the way the bugs lit up the countryside and let out a breath.

"I know, but there has to be a loophole or something."

"Are you telling me you believe the Big Man forgot to cover all the angles? That you're going to figure out a way to outsmart ..." She pointed upward toward the ceiling.

"Judas did not say God made the Horsemen."

"No, just every biblical teaching ever printed does. They may be a neutral force, but He created them and the two of us are not going to find the virtual back door to hack the system."

"Fine." Frustration caused us both to raise our voices, but I didn't care. "What, then? We sit here and enjoy our drinks and a little chit chat? Maybe we could bring in a TV and watch the Topside action live. I'll bet that would really pack the Woebegone into this place."

Alex glared at me with eyes that said I had better check myself before she did it for me.

"Sorry. I know you're as frustrated as I am." I pounded a fist onto the bar making our half full cans rattle. "I just don't know what to do."

Alex's expression softened and her eyes told a story of sadness and defeat as well.

"I don't know either. Do we get any perks as a Denarii Agent? Anything we could use to maybe help out on the sidelines up there?"

I let out a humorless laugh. "Yeah, your coin will turn into all sorts of crazy things to confuse and confound you."

Alex raised an eyebrow in question but didn't say anything.

"Do you remember that time you almost killed me in the alley when we were Topside doing security for Nick's big announcement about finding the cure for cancer? And I had to hide behind a dumpster so you wouldn't shoot me?"

"Yeah." She put a hand on my shoulder. "Sorry about that."

"And remember I told you ghosts were responsible?"

"I remember you waving your arms around like a lunatic and walking around in a one-legged pair of pants." She raised an eyebrow.

"Well, the ghosts were called Whisper Wraiths, and they were everywhere trying to cause problems. I couldn't talk about it without divulging the secret of the coin." I turned toward her and leaned an elbow on the bar. "It's nice to be able to explain all of this, but I think you secretly enjoyed the pants."

Alex snorted and I continued.

"Anyway, when the Whisper Wraiths showed up, the coin

turned into an invisible giant flaming axe. I could fight the wraiths but—"

"You looked like a raving lunatic." She finished the sentence for me. "And the flames burned away half your pants. And you're right, I'm not complaining." She winked. "Have you ever considered assless chaps?"

I rolled my eyes and went on. "And the weird flashlight that would show War even when she was camouflaged."

Alex's eyes went wide with realization.

"Right. And do you remember when we first met, and we put a stop to Max and Jake's plan to infect the Olympic games? That time it gave me the super weird power to smell their awful durian fruit from half a mile away."

Alex smacked me on the arm. "You blamed me for that smell."

I laughed. "Yeah, but that was before I knew how the coin worked. For the record, I'm glad it wasn't you. I don't think I could work with someone who emitted a smell like that."

She smacked me again and this time let her hand fall on my thigh. "You still couldn't resist me." She smiled and squeezed my knee.

Her touch was electric. It distracted me from everything we had been talking about. So, when she asked what the coin had done for me this time, she caught me a bit off guard.

"I mean if I'm hearing you right, the coin provides you with the tool you need to succeed, right. So, what did it provide when we faced Simeon and Jake?"

I sat there dumbfounded for a moment. She was right. I had not been in possession of the coin until Judas gave it back to me. Alex had mine, but it should have done something—unless.

"Maybe we really aren't meant to interfere with the Horsemen."

Alex tilted her head in surprise at that.

"I hadn't thought of it before now, but you're right. The coin provides an agent with the tool he or she needs to succeed. Judas said it's a power granted straight from the top. The real top."

Now it was my turn to point toward the Heavens. "If we were meant to stop or even involve ourselves with the fight against the Horsemen, it should have provided us with something. You had the coin the whole time and Judas gave me one too."

I pulled the Denarius out of my pocket and looked at it.

"Maybe this is a sign that we're supposed to stand by and let this thing happen."

Alex peered at my hand, staring at the coin as well. Neither of us said a word as reality set in. Then before either of us could respond, the coin flashed a bright green, burning the flesh on my palm.

I threw the coin to the ground out of instinct, but it was already changing. The coin elongated and grew, forming a crooked black staff. I recognized the shape even before the blade began to form at the top. The metal looked pitted and old, but the edge was as deadly as ever. The newly transformed implement lay on the floor all but humming with power. The coin had answered after all. It had become the one thing we needed. The last mantle to bring Death upon the world of humanity.

CHAPTER TWENTY-FIVE

I slid off my stool and inched over to where the sickle lay on the ground. It looked much larger than I remembered. The staff had to be more than six feet in length and the long, curved blade at least two thirds as long as the staff. It was black and ancient looking, but when I stared at it, the wicked looking weapon almost seemed to emit a sickly green aura. It called to me, and I could not help but answer. I reached toward the shaft, trembling with expectation, then another force, this one much more violent and visceral hit me from the side.

I was taken off my feet like a wide receiver trying to recover a fumbled football and flailed in the air a moment before coming down hard with Alex on top of me. I fought out of reflex as she scrambled to straddle my torso and pin my arms to the ground.

"What the literal freak are you doing?" I scowled at her, giving up the fight for the moment in order to extract some sort of answer.

She blinked, mouth half open, sheer panic in her eyes. "That may have been a slight over reaction."

"Slight?"

"I didn't want you to touch that thing." Her blue hair hung

over her face in a way that was not at all sexy and arousing as she straddled my body.

"You could have just said, hey wait, don't touch that thing."

She put her hand on my cheek. "I know, I'm sorry."

"If you two are done flirting I'm turning into a duck pancake down here." Quack's voice broke into our head sounding garbled and muffled as if he spoke through a pillow. He never talked out loud so it made no sense that his voice would sound different.

I rolled Alex and I over in a rush to get Quack out from under my back. He had been pinned inside my backpack during Alex's surprise attack, and in all the excitement I had forgotten about him.

"Are you all right?" I gently shrugged out of the backpack and opened the top to peek inside. To my relief Quack popped his head out, then bit down on my finger.

"Ouch." I jerked my hand out of the way.

"Next time you and the blue hair decide to roll in the hay, take your backpack off first."

"It wasn't my fault. Alex attacked me. I didn't have a choice."

"That's what they all say." Quack lumbered the rest of the way out of the bag and stretched his wings. "What a rude way to wake up from a nap. What did I miss? What is that thing?"

Quack began to waddle toward the sickle, but I shot forward and scooped him up before he touched it and became the world's first Death duck.

"That is not for you, no matter what."

"Fine." He quacked out loud. "You don't have to be so handsy."

Alex and I both got up and I put Quack on the bar out of harm's way.

"Okay, you have successfully prevented me from touching the sickle—for now. What did you want to say?"

Alex turned a sideways glance toward the wicked looking implement on the floor.

"I don't know. What if it works? What if it doesn't? What if you turn into Death and I can't get you back? Maybe we haven't thought this thing through."

I reached out and clasped Alex by her shoulders.

"This will work ... I think. I do know one thing for sure. If I wasn't meant to pick that thing up it wouldn't be here. Don't forget who controls the coin. This is definitely treading the line between good and evil as far as meddling with a neutral force, but if the coin is flashing a green light this bright, I don't see how we can ignore it."

Alex looked at me and sighed. "All right. But you better stay Gabe, or Horsemen or not, you'll have me to deal with." She reached out and clasped my hand in hers. "I just got you back. I was getting used to having you around again."

I pulled Alex close and kissed her. She wrapped her arms around me and kissed back, sending waves of strength ... and doubt throughout my body.

When we parted, I peered at her again and smiled. "If I become anything but Gabe, I expect you to come after me. I can't think of anything more terrifying."

Alex laughed and turned her eyes toward the sickle again.

"Ok. Go get this over with before I change my mind."

I let go of her, took a breath and stepped toward the mantle. I hesitated only a moment, then reached out and took it up, feeling the power of Death course through me.

CHAPTER TWENTY-SIX

Traveling Topside to fight the Horsemen without Alex felt wrong. She had been a part of this from the beginning. She was a member of the Denarii Division, not to mention my partner. Being here by myself felt lonely and more than a little unnerving. I thought I would feel different, carrying the mantle of Death. The other Horsemen seemed to struggle with some sort of force that overtook them. I felt ... well, nothing. After the initial infusion of power, it was like I hadn't changed at all. The more I thought about it, the more I became convinced the coin had failed to produce a true mantle. But then I caught a glimpse of my reflection in what was left of a Times Square display window.

My face looked gaunt and skeletal, as if I hadn't eaten since the invention of Twinkies. My body, however had benefited from a healthy dose of lean sinewy muscle, not that I could see it under my new Death garb. Gone were my t-shirt and jeans. Instead, I wore a ragged, hooded cloak; dark, weathered and heavy, like a midnight storm cloud. A formidable pairing to my new equestrian nightmare.

Half flesh and half rotting skeleton, my horse showed blackened and yellowing portions of its skull and ribs. Spiderwebs filled the voids where organs should go and the beast's eyes glowed orange with the literal flames of Hell. The hide that did show was a pale white; powerful and muscular but at the same time furtive and empty. I decided to call him Hollow. A good name, and he didn't seem to hate it. At least he didn't try to trample me when I said it, so I took it as a good sign.

I held the sickle in my left hand, the butt secured in the stirrup, so the blade swept out to my side like a morbid banner. Hollow came to a halt as I tugged on the reins and looked around. I never visited Time Square while I was alive, but I had seen photos. The place I saw before me now bore no resemblance to the pictures.

Glass littered the ground, and the air held the scent of smoke and rot. There were no flashing lights or glittering billboards. No people, no vendors or bright yellow cabs. Empty shells of automobiles and busses crisscrossed the street as makeshift barriers. Some burning, some not. Trash blew everywhere and I could see piles of appliances stacked up as gun emplacements. There weren't as many bodies as I had seen in Denver, but they were here too. Perhaps the fighting had lulled enough for people to collect and care for their dead ... if they even had the mind left to do so.

"Hey, Hop Along Cadaver. You want to slow down a little. Flying with these new wings isn't easy."

I glanced up to see Quack glide in for a landing. More of a crash landing ... a collision course with my chest. Quack flapped his wings like a hummingbird after an all you can eat buffet binge. I reached out to catch him like a flopping feathery football.

"Thanks. I guess my approach still needs some work."

Quack's transformation was not unanticipated due to our soul bond, but I did hope the mantle would have a minimal effect on him. I was wrong. He had not taken on the full undead personas like my mount, but his feathers had become ragged and the blue-black color of his legs and webbed feet and bill had turned to a bleached bone white, making him look as if he were truly a duck of the dead.

"So, have you figured out this power thing yet? I've been trying to do things all day. I snuck up on a pigeon and gave it the old death touch, but nothing happened. Maybe there's a trick to it. Do you think I have to be holding the sickle? Can I borrow it for a few minutes? I'll bring it right back, I swear."

I set Quack in front of me, letting him rest on the sun-bleached saddle.

"How are you planning to hold it? You don't have thumbs."

"I could sort of balance it on my beak or stand on it until a pigeon flies close enough for me to touch. We could put out some bird seed or bread to attract them. Come to think of it, I'm pretty hungry. Do you have any bread?"

I heeled Hollow into a slow walk. "No, I don't have any bread and it's bad for you. Go use your superpowers to kill some bugs and eat those."

"Very funny. I could do that already. Where are we going, anyway? I thought we were headed for a big showdown or something."

"I'm looking for War. And I hope she'll be in the mood to talk now that we're on more of a level playing field."

"Talk? That doesn't sound very apocalyptic."

"I don't care how it sounds. There's been enough fighting and death. If I can talk her out of this madness, she might help me with the others too."

"Ah." Quack nodded his little feathery head. "Gathering allies. Good plan."

"Can you be quiet for a second? I can sort of sense her. I think it's one of our powers. She's close but it's hard to concentrate when you're jabbering away like that."

"Well excuse me Mr. Death. Figures, you get all powered up

and it goes straight to your head. Maybe I can sense her too. Did you ever think of that? Did you ever think to ask me what I felt?"

I jerked on the reigns yanking Hollow to a halt as a huge hulking figure emerged from an alley fifty yards ahead of us. Quack had to flap his wings to maintain his balance on the saddle.

"What's wrong with you? You could warn a duck before you do something like that."

He turned his head and peered up the street. "Oh, there she is. I told you I could sense her. You should have just asked me earlier."

"Why don't you fly above us and stay out of harm's way until we see how she's going to react to us being here."

Quack nodded. "I think that's a good idea. How about a little boost?"

I tore my eyes away from War and glanced down at him.

"Boost?"

"Yeah, you know. Like an aircraft carrier. Give me a launch. Throw me into the air."

I sighed. "Fine."

I scooped him up and turned him away from me.

"Okay now do a countdown from ten. Ten, nine ..."

I tossed him into the air as hard as I thought I could without hurting him.

"Zero, you were supposed to go on zero. Who taught you to count?"

I ignored Quack as he flapped his wings and gained altitude, flying out of the danger zone. Now all I had to do was reason with the homicidal maniac at the end of the street.

I raised a hand in greeting and hoped she would do the same, but War just sat on her huge battle armored mount staring at me, clutching her broken ebony broadsword. I had forgotten how menacing she looked. All clad in crimson armor with a skull shielded helmet. She still wore her cloaking cape that concealed her from mortal eyes but now that I had joined the Horseman club, I could see her without a problem.

"I only want to talk," I shouted.

She remained a good distance away, but there was no noise to dampen my words either. In fact, I was a little unnerved by the lack of battle sounds. Had she induced some sort of ceasefire? If so, why? Did she know I was coming? Could she sense me as well? Sense me better than I could sense her? All these questions left me at a distinct disadvantage, but I couldn't think about that now.

I heeled Hollow into a slow walk, moving in her direction. "You and I can take the first step toward ending this thing. We don't have to do this. All you have to do is resist the power of the mantle."

War turned her mount to face me and heeled it into a walk as well. For a moment I thought she might be ready to talk. Then she raised her ebony broadsword and kicked her heels, urging her mount into a charge.

I pulled my mount to stop again doing everything I could to appear non-threatening. "I only want to talk."

Watching her charge at me brought on a wave of emotion. Images of her pounding the bus as I tried to escape, leading thousands of people to their deaths in battle and most of all, the memory of her plunging her massive broadsword into my chest. A strange mix of fear and fury threatened to overwhelm me, but I seized on the latter and arced the blade of my sickle over to parry War's blow as she charged by. Our blades crashed with an ear-rending ring sending blue-white sparks into the air. I could hear the hooves of War's mount grinding to a halt behind me, struggling to turn for another strike, but I was not about to offer her another free shot.

I yanked Hollow around and he whinnied and huffed with excitement, lurching into a dead run. War was slower to recover. I attacked before she could face me and fully block my blow. My sickle arced out with far more range than her broadsword, giving it more momentum as well. She took part of the hit on the flat of her sword, but the blow threw her off balance and breached her thick armor. When I turned for another run, she was already advancing on me. This time I saw she was hurt.

I pressed my advantage and feigned another strike but at the last moment brought my sickle around before me like a lance. She tried to bring her sword up to block, rearing her horse back to stop but it was too late. The butt end of my sickle hit her square in the chest, toppling her backward and throwing her from her horse in a crash of heavy armor and steel. Her mount slowed to a stop and turned to retrieve her, but I used Hollow to block its path, managing a swift dismount of my own.

I hoped my horse would be as intuitive as hers and keep the warhorse busy while I finished my business with its rider. War lay face down on the ground, her helmet knocked free to reveal long locks of matted blond hair. I raised my sickle ready to strike. This would end now, one way or another. Either she would yield, or I would ensure she never had a chance to raise her armies again.

"It's over. Throw away your sword and turn around."

She lifted her head off the dirt but did not face me. Nor did she release her sword. I stood over her while she lay motionless on the asphalt clutching her weapon. Was she trying to decide what to do? Gathering the courage to lash out with one last suicidal strike? Then it hit me ... Literally.

I heard the report of the rifle a fraction of a second after the shell hit me in the back. Someone had fired at me. Then I felt the sting of another bullet, then another and another, like giant wasps against my skin. Within the span of a breath, I was under the fire of hundreds, maybe thousands of guns. Mortal weapons could not kill a Niner, but I wasn't really a Niner anymore. I had no real idea what rules applied. My mantle seemed to work in much the same way, healing Topside inflicted wounds in an instant, but overcoming thousands of gunshots would stretch the limits of even a Niner's invincibility health plan. So many attacks at once were impossible to ignore. The pain was all but unbearable. I tried to strike out at War, thinking I could end the attack by stopping her, but my swing was weak and impotent. I fell to my knees under the pressure and weight of so many shots. Still, the gunfire continued. I kept my eyes on War. She seemed to tremble with effort, and though she had not moved from her spot on the ground, I was about to crumble under the weight of her armies.

I fell to my hands and knees as I concentrated on repelling the gunfire. A growl of defiance ground out of my throat. I could not lose this fight ... would not lose this fight again. There had to be something more. Death could not be defeated by mortal weapons. Something inside me tore loose. Something sickly and foreign broke free like a wave and rushed to my aid. Power coursed through me as this new ability took shape and I began to laugh. Its sheer potential washed over me like a torrent of warm inequity. At first nothing happened, but they were coming. I had called, and they would heed my command. War's troops closed in as well. They fired out in the open now. I saw assault weapons, pistols and huge hunting rifles with scopes, but it didn't matter. My legions approached and guns were no match for the dead.

The first ghostly figure streaked onto the battlefield from a side street, shrieking its arrival for all to hear. Some of the gunmen turned and tried to shoot it down but their bullets passed right through. Within seconds every street was bloated with wraiths; ghostly apparitions that poured in like fog, attacking with incorporeal madness. War's troops turned their guns away from me and tried to defend themselves. Their guns were useless. The wraiths smothered, blinded, and maimed their prey with ferocious efficiency. The chill they brought with them froze many of the attackers to the bone and others were driven mad with fear. War's line was broken in seconds, and I was back on my feet, looming among it all. The true power of Death's mantle seemed almost limitless, and I had but dipped a hand into the pool. I could not fathom the depths of this dark ocean and I feared to even look at the waters.

I raised my sickle one last time, ready to end this madness. War collapsed in defeat, turning onto her back to face me. I swung my sickle down to harvest her soul but then I saw her face. Horror seized me and I altered my swing to graze her cheek, drawing a line of blood from her bruised and filthy face. I tossed my weapon to the ground and knelt beside her, staring into her wild eyes.

"What are you doing here?"

CHAPTER TWENTY-EIGHT

I stood, holding Hollow's bridle as I waited outside an old warehouse on the outskirts of the city. It was an old brick building with windows too high to peek into unless you had a six-foot ladder in your hip pocket. The place was abandoned like so many others in the area. The owners probably out fighting ... or dead.

I had never seen anyone appear in through a splice point before. There was no flash or noise. No unusual sensory que to announce their arrival. They were absent one second, then there the next. Like when a stranger bumped into you from behind. If I hadn't been staring in the precise spot where they landed, it would have looked like they walked in and I had simply missed their approach. I could see how people dismissed it as something else.

Alex spotted me and hurried over to where I stood.

"I got your message. This had better be important. Do you have any idea how much trouble I would be in if we got caught doing this?"

I glanced at our other two guests. Meg and Jazzy. They had not just helped when I wandered The Nine without my memories; they were like family, and right now we needed all the family we could get. Unfortunately, said family was bent over in a side bush hurling out their lunch. I sympathized. There was no experience quite so gut wrenching as your first splice trip.

"Trust me. This is a big one."

"Gabe, is that you?" Jazzy stood, wiping her face on her sleeve. Meg followed suit and the two of them seemed to take in the whole picture, undead horse, sickle and all.

"Wait a minute." Meg held out an arm, barring Jazzy from getting any closer. "What is this? You look like ..."

She paused, stopping short of saying the last word.

"Death?" I finished. "Yeah, I've been getting that a lot lately."

I turned to Alex.

"You didn't fill them in on anything before you came up?"

Alex shrugged. "You said to hurry. I hurried. It was hard enough to explain how we were going Topside."

I sighed and turned to the stunned looking duo still standing several feet away.

"Let me explain." I paused for a second, then shook my head. "No, there is too much, let me sum up. The Four Horsemen are loose here on earth. Someone set the wakeup call a little early, so I became Death to stop the other three. I've captured War. She's inside this warehouse and that's why you're all here. I've hit a snag and I need your help. If you'ill just ignore ..." I gestured to myself and the demonic looking horse, "this, and go in, you'll see why."

Jazzy and Meg stared at me for a minute then Meg dropped her arm.

"Good enough for me. Let's go."

Meg stepped toward me and Jazzy followed, both wearing familiar grins on their faces.

"This is not a good look for you, by the way." Jazzy pointed to my frayed cloak. "Did you get that thing off a homeless guy or what?"

"I don't know." Meg eyed me up and down as well. "I sort of like it. It's very, Merlin the Magician." She patted my chest causing a cloud of dust. "It's a little long though, and it could use a dry cleaner. And what's with this sickle? Do you have to carry this around all the time?"

"All right." I batted her hand away. "Thank you for the fashion critique. Can we go inside now? This is important."

"Sure," Meg said, as they parted. "Lead the way."

Alex smirked at me as I tugged my mount into motion.

"Not a word from you either."

I let the sickle fall limp at my side, carrying it more like a lunch box than a massive weapon of death and led them toward a garage door. I reached into my pocket and hit a button and the door began to move. The moment it was up, I led everyone inside, including my horse, then hit the button to shut the door again.

"Hey, wait for me." Before the door could close all the way, a feathery black cannon ball came blasting in through the doorway. Quack came to a skidding stop several feet past where we stood then waddled back again.

"What, were you just going to close the door on me?"

"I wouldn't dream of it."

I turned to lead the three women into the warehouse without saying anything else, leaving my mount standing next to the door.

"You were going to leave me out there. I can't believe it. Well, I'm just going to stand over here in the nonhuman section. Your horse is better company anyway."

I wanted to respond, even apologize but I could not afford any more distractions. This was too important. I needed to find a solution to this problem and fast, or I would not be able to face

Simeon and Jake to stop their campaign as the other two Horsemen.

I continued further into the warehouse. War stood with her back to us as we approached, and we all gave her a wide berth as we circled around. I had her chained to a heavy piece of machinery. Her armor seemed to be a part of her. Removing it would be like removing her skin, so I had to leave it on. Her helmet was off though, and I had her sword on the far side of the room, out of her reach. I made sure she couldn't get to it and command her troops. War had been captured and she was alone, but nothing was ever that simple.

"Zoe?" Jazzy recognized her first and ran over, but I reached out to block her just before she got within reach of Zoe's teeth.

Zoe was like a daughter to me, I had saved her from a firestorm as a Freshborn, nursed her to health and we had become more than friends. She took over running my shop and had become part of my family. Then she took vengeance on an entire nightclub in The Nine, killing everyone inside, innocent or not. She disappeared after that. I should have been there ... should have stopped her. When no one heard from her, we all feared the worst. None of us could have imagined this.

Zoe lashed out, trying to bite anyone within reach, struggling against the chains that bound her arms and legs.

"What did you do to her?" Meg glared at me with accusing eyes.

"I only captured her." I let go of Jazzy as soon as I was sure she wouldn't try to get too close. "But that is not Zoe. That's War. The mantle has taken her over completely. I think ... I believe Zoe is still in there. That's why I brought all of you here. I tried to talk to her, but I think all she sees is this."

I gestured to my Grim Reaper fashion accessories.

"To her, I'm Death and she is War, nothing more than that. I'm hoping she will recognize your faces. The three of you were inseparable before she disappeared. She loves you two. You're as close to her as I was ... I am. If she recognizes you, maybe Zoe can ... I don't know, regain control somehow."

"I remember you." The voice that came out of War did not sound at all like Zoe. It was more visceral and clipped. Like the voice of a madwoman ranting on the street. To my surprise, her eyes were on Alex, not Meg or Jazzy. "You are the one who wields fire. I missed you, but I got your friend." She let out a stream of maniacal laughter.

Alex let it die down then pointed to me. "Looks to me like you didn't do a very good job."

Zoe's eyes flicked in my direction and her grin turned to a snarl. She lashed out again, trying to get loose, biting, growling and spitting at Alex.

"You shouldn't upset her like that."

The familiar voice came from the shadows, and I turned to see Sammy walk into the light.

"What are you doing here?" Alex scowled at Sammy. "Don't you have something better to do than track us down and get in our business."

Sammy ignored her jibe and returned a genuine smile. "You are far more important to me than anything else. Especially right now. I fear you are making one grave mistake after the other." She cast a glance in my direction. "No pun intended. Love the wardrobe change by the way."

I offered her a tight-lipped smile. "Thanks, but I think we can handle things here." I tried to return her friendly tone but even I was a little annoyed at the earthbound angel's intrusion.

Alex turned her back on Sammy to focus on Zoe with Meg and Jazzy. The best thing I could do was serve as a distraction while they tried to coax our old friend out of hiding.

"So, what can we do for you?"

I headed Sammy off before she could get too close and walked her in the opposite direction. By the way she kept her eyes on Zoe and the others I could tell she was not happy about the detour, but she smiled and complied anyway.

"I'm not here for my sake. I'm here for yours." Her eyes kept flicking to Zoe and the girls but I pretended not to notice. "I only want to dissuade you from involving yourself in this any further. You must see that trying to stop this can only make it worse."

She stepped back and took me in for the first time.

"Take you for instance. You've taken the mantle of Death and put yourself on a path that cannot be denied. The hunger must feel all consuming."

I looked at her trying to figure what she played at.

She stepped forward again and lowered her voice to a tone only I could hear. Something seductive and surreal.

"You must feel the call. The mantle is not a weapon for you to wield like some trinket retrieved from a battlefield. *You* are the tool. Your hands have become the weapons."

Sammy reached out and put a hand on my arm, urging me to raise the sickle I had been holding down by my side. I butted the end to the floor with a hollow sounding thud allowing the blade to sweep out over our heads.

"You were meant to wield this mantle just as War was meant to wield hers. Return her sword. Set her free. Only after her tasks are complete can Zoe be returned to herself again."

I nodded. Suddenly everything made sense. If War finished her job, Zoe would be free to return. Maybe the shock of having her mantle would even allow Zoe to come forth and take control.

I walked over to where I had propped the sword into a corner, safe from War's grasp. I picked it up and went to return it to its rightful owner.

"What do you think you're doing?"

Alex had moved in behind me making me jump the moment I turned around. She had her hands on her hips, glowering like a scolding mother who caught her child scribbling on the walls with a purple crayon.

"I need to return this?" The words even sounded ridiculous to me. What had I been thinking? Why would I give Zoe her sword? My mind felt foggy and full of mud. I couldn't remember what happened. I just remembered talking to Sammy, then I decided to come over here and ...

Before I could take that line of reasoning any further, something else caught my attention. The locket I wore around my neck. I had inherited it from desperate Woebegone woman in The Nine and kept it safe ever since. Alex and I discovered it was an object of great power. Something called an Origin Artifact. It had the ability to create or alter some element of The Nine. We didn't know precisely what it did, but it had saved my life by bonding my broken soul to Quack. In doing so, we were bonded as one and my soul was saved from everlasting oblivion.

Now the locket grew hot. So hot it began to glow orange beneath my cloak. I smelled burning cotton and more urgently, burning flesh. I dropped War's broadsword and pulled the locket away from my skin, but it was already beginning to cool. The moment I let go of the sword the heat subsided.

I stared at Alex and she stared back. We both looked down at the sword and I could tell she had come to the same conclusion I had. It was worth a shot anyway. What could it hurt?

I slipped the locket off my neck and marched straight toward Zoe. Alex did not move with me. She must have known something I had not yet recognized.

"No!" It was Sammy. She charged in behind me, but Alex got in her way. It gave me just enough time to reach Zoe.

She screamed as well, stretching her bound hand as much as she could toward the fallen broadsword. Her eyes were full of panic and desperation. Zoe thrashed and fought harder than she had since she arrived, but the chains held fast and I placed the locket against her forehead, willing it to life. The moment I did, the locket glowed with bright white light and Zoe went stiff. Her eyes went wide and then her body seemed to melt out of the armor, becoming more of a withered core within a shell.

With the task complete, the locket dimmed and then went dark again. Zoe hung there, unconscious, but I knew War had retreated and disappeared. She was our friend, the dear and beloved member of our family. Meg and Jazzy ran over to Zoe. I tossed them the key for the locks on the chains. Now that Zoe was herself again, we had to get her home. That and find out why a treacherous angel seemed bent on destroying the world.

CHAPTER TWENTY-NINE

I rounded on the angel who stood several paces behind us. She panted with anger and frustration. She clenched her fists at her side and her head was lowered in an unholy gesture of aggressive hatred and fury.

"What have you done?"

"I think that is a question better suited to you." I stepped toward her, moving Alex behind me, butting my sickle to the ground. I wanted to be sure I was between her and any wrath she might visit upon the room.

"Give me five minutes alone with her in pigeon form." Quack waddled up beside me, apparently bored with the more equestrian side of the team. "I'll tear her limb from feather."

His eyes burned a glowing orange, and I did not need a mirror to know mine did the same. While I usually took his comments as off the cuff aggravation, this time I knew he meant every word.

"Why would you do something like this?" I asked, hoping Quack would take the hint and hold his ground. "You're on the books as one of the good guys."

Sammy huffed out a laugh. "I didn't orchestrate this coup.

Though, I did pitch the idea. And your superiors on The Council were all too eager to jump on board. Besides, the people here deserve it."

"You have no right to pass judgement." Alex moved to stand just behind me. I was grateful she took my defensive cue. "You may think you're God, but trust me, you fall way short on qualifications."

"I have no right?" Sammy spat the words and for a second, I thought she might try to strike at Alex. Instead, she relegated herself to glaring at her then turned her daggers on me.

"I lived among the filth of humanity for countless generations. Consigned to this existence by the Father, and for what? To watch you piss away every gift, every blessing bestowed upon this world and your filthy species. Humans poison this planet, exploit every resource, you murder, cheat, rape, and defile one another. You are treacherous creatures who know nothing of the true gifts you have been given. I witnessed the acts of Hitler and Vlad the Impaler and Saddam Hussain first-hand. I had a ringside seat to Hiroshima and 9/11. I saw it all. I watched it happen. I dwelled among you, always watching, always waiting, never interfering, never rebuking not until now. Now you will all reap the reward for your hatred and greed. You will know the hand of true wrath and not even God can do anything to stop it."

"So, this is all just a case of, *I think I'm smarter than my boss*?" I sneered. "You realize you're only here because He allowed you to be here. You can't even go anywhere else. You're a bitter supernatural with a chip on her shoulder because daddy put you in a corner. Just because you stand in your little bubble and watch the world go by doesn't mean you understand it."

Alex moved next to me. "You see the bad parts because you want to. You've decided humanity is corrupt or immoral so that's what you look for. You talk about Hitler and Hiroshima but what you're doing is so much worse. You close your eyes to the light and turn your back on anything good. You don't deserve to be called angel. You're every villain you claim to detest all rolled into one."

I saw Sammy's fury building and I took another step forward. "What are you hoping to gain from all of this? A trip to Heaven? After all you've done to His favorite children?"

I chose my words carefully and the edge cut deep. Sammy responded by doing something even I found terrifying. She smiled.

"And I thought you understood. As I said, your kind has no grasp on the true blessings of the Father. Highest among them is forgiveness."

That threw me for a moment. She was right. The big man was forgiving to a fault, though I had a hard time believing he could overlook something like this.

Alex let out a low chuckle that drew all our attention. When I looked at her, she had triumph written all over her face.

"There you go again," she said. "Thinking you've outsmarted the Boss. You're forgetting one thing. To be forgiven you must be truly repentant. You have to be sorry and *mean* it. No matter how you flower your apology, He will know the truth."

I looked to Sammy and saw that Alex's words had cut far deeper than mine. The enraged angel lashed out with her hand, manifesting a flaming gladius. The room burst to light with its power, and I felt the heat of its flame. She charged forward to attack and I moved to cut her off. As she brought her gladius down, I swung the blade of my sickle around to meet it. The two inerrable forces clashed with a boom. The gladius went no further.

Sammy stood, staring at the point where our weapons met in utter astonishment, shocked that her weapon had not destroyed me.

"Whether you're working for good or bad you cannot stand against the will of a Horseman." I paused and let the words sink in for a moment. "Continue on this course and my will shall be to destroy you."

Sammy's gaze shifted to my eyes with sheer hatred.

"You will not be able to resist the mantle forever. You will fall to its power and bring about the Apocalypse. I will have my vengeance on humanity whether I return to Heaven or not."

With that, she withdrew and burst into a cloud of pigeons and rose into the air, escaping through a broken window before Quack had a chance to exact his own vengeance on her avian form.

CHAPTER THIRTY

I walked Jazzy, Meg and Alex back to their splice point, leading Hollow with Quack perched on the saddle like a mighty Hun warrior. I was pretty sure Sammy had gotten the message, but I didn't want her to pop in and exact her revenge while I wasn't around, or worse, acquire War's mantle.

Alex had it wrapped in an old blanket, tied at the ends with a length of used rope, like a sort of makeshift messenger bag. She had slung it across her back so no one could touch it, not even her.

Jazzy and Meg walked a few paces ahead of us pushing Zoe in a squeaky wheelchair we found in the warehouse. The previous owner must have had a miraculous story to tell, or they opted for a better set of wheels. Either way, I was grateful for the discovery. Zoe was still unconscious, and it meant we didn't have to carry her to the splice point like a sack of rice.

The two seemed none the worse for wear considering the enormity of all they had witnessed. The Nine could be crazy, but watching Death and an Angel from Heaven duke it out in a warehouse next to a friend who had become the Horseman, War? That was a whole other wing in the nuthouse.

"I need you to do something for me when you get back to the agency." I kept my voice low so only Alex could hear me.

She glanced up, raising an eyebrow, inviting me to continue.

"I want you to hide this sword. Go to Judas if you need to. Hide it in a place no one can ever find it." I hesitated then finished. "Especially me."

"You? What are you talking about? You saved Zoe and separated her from the sword. Why would I need to hide it from you?"

I scowled at her, not wanting to explain, but she kept staring at me, demanding an answer.

"It's a precaution. In case ..." I hesitated, not wanting to say it out loud. Both, because I didn't want it to happen, but more because I didn't want Sammy to have the satisfaction of being right.

"In case he goes full psycho Death on everyone." Quack broke into our conversations with his usual eloquent demeanor. "He doesn't want to be able to steal the sword back."

"Thanks Quack." I thought at him. "I can handle this."

"Fine." He huffed. "I was just trying to help."

I turned to Alex and stammered. "But yes. Pretty much exactly that."

Alex's expression turned to a cat's grin. "Good."

"Good?" I screwed up my face in confusion. "What's good? What do you mean good?"

Alex snorted out a little laugh. Oh, how I wished I could just sit and listen to her laugh.

"I wanted to hear you say it. I don't want you running around thinking you're immune to the mantle's power. You better remember how dangerous this is. I want you coming back to me and not as some grim reaper. When this is over, I want Gabe, just the way he was before this whole thing started."

I smiled and let out a little laugh of my own. "I really want to kiss you right now."

She held a hand between us. "The kiss of Death? No thanks. Save it for later. Let's make an agreement that all affection is on hold until you're no longer the dark harvester of souls."

I tried to laugh that one off but couldn't quite get it out.

"What is it?" Alex noticed the waver in my step and looked at me with concern.

I glanced up to see that Jazzy and Meg still pushed Zoe along the abandoned city sidewalk ahead of us, holding their own conversation, oblivious to ours.

"It's something that happened during our fight. Between Zoe and me."

"What do you mean." Alex shrugged. "Zoe's in one piece, you're not hurt. I can't imagine things going any better."

"It's not the two of us that I am worried about."

Alex didn't say anything else, giving me time to order my thoughts.

"During our fight. While Zoe was still entranced by War I mean, I had won; I overpowered her, but then she turned her troops on me. I couldn't handle her and hundreds of guns at the same time."

I saw the growing concern on Alex's face even though she knew I had come out of the ordeal on one piece.

"What did you do? How did you defend yourself against that many people?"

"That's just it. I didn't. Well, not me, alone." I took a breath, remembering the vision of what I had created on that battlefield. "Somehow this mantle gives me the power to raise the dead. I can raise the spirits and form an army of wraiths to fight for me."

That set Alex back a few steps. "Well, that's awesome. I don't see why that's a bad thing. That could come in pretty handy when you fight Simeon and his Snot Zombies."

"Yes." I paused. "But I'm already dead. The people fighting here in the U.S. aren't. Nor are the people under Simeon's control. They are all innocents being used as puppets by one of the Horsemen. How can I bring my wraiths to bear against them when they are nothing but victims themselves?"

Alex shook her head. "I don't know. Maybe you have some other power that you can use against him. Or get him alone so it's a fair fight one on one."

I laughed. "Something tells me Simeon is not one for a fair fight, and if I have some ability more powerful than that one, I'm not sure I want to know what it is."

Alex was about to say something else when I heard another familiar voice ahead of us. We both looked toward Jazzy and Meg and saw Zoe stir.

I tugged on Hollow's bridle, and we hurried forward. We were almost to the splice point, but I wanted to be able to talk to her before they left. I had so much to say. So much to apologize for. We had parted on such poor terms. I should have never let her go. Never let her take such a violent and vengeful path. She was my friend and I had watched her walk out of my life without so much as a shout or an argument to try and stop her. I could never forgive myself for that.

When I walked around to face Zoe in her wheelchair, I found the words would not come. Only tears threatened to express my happiness ... and regret. I tried to start a sentence several times, but while my mouth moved, no sound would follow. Zoe had no such trouble.

"Wow you look like crap."

The honest profession was all it took to bring about a gale of laughter from everyone standing around her.

"Zoe, I'm sorry." I started to say when the laughter died down. She held up a hand to stop me.

"You have nothing to apologize for. I'm the one who's sorry. You were nothing but good to me. You all were, but my vengeance led me all the way into this."

She gestured to the abandoned city around us.

"Granted most people would not sink quite this low but I'm not one to do things halfway."

Another chuckle from everyone, this one less enthusiastic.

"I'm sorry. To all of you. But especially you Gabe. If there's ever anything I can do to make it up to you, all you need to do is ask. I owe you more than I could ever repay. I owe you the lives of everyone who died because of my selfishness."

Tears began to flow over her cheeks, and I wanted to reach down and embrace her, but I feared what would happen if I touched anyone with my power. Alex seemed to key into this and leaned down to hug her instead, followed by Jazzy then Meg.

They all crouched there in that awkward position for several seconds, crying together, not at all making me cry or wipe away silent tears before any of them stood and saw me. I was Death after all. The Grim Reaper did not cry.

When they all straightened, everyone smiled in thoughtful concern then looked back to me.

"Are you going to be okay?" Alex asked.

I nodded. "I'll head out after Simeon next. If I can catch him off guard, maybe I can separate him from his mantle without a fight or at least without hurting more people."

Alex nodded, but I doubted she believed sneaking up on Simeon was any more possible than I did.

"Get to The Nine and lay low. I'm glad you're okay, Zoe." I looked at her again. She hadn't even tried to get out of her wheelchair. The ordeal as War must have taken more out of her than she led on. "As soon as I get back, you and I will catch up."

Zoe nodded. "Deal. Just make sure you come back in one piece."

I looked at Alex and answered. "That's a promise."

With that, the four of them turned and disappeared like a cloud of mist. Another first for me. Seeing them disappear into the splice point felt a little surreal. They were returning without me, and I was alone once again. Well, sort of alone.

"Let's get this show on the road. I'm ready to do some serious butt kicking." Quack flapped in Hollow's saddle, punctuating his point.

"I'm glad you're excited. If we're going to take Simeon down, we're going to need all the enthusiasm we can get."

CHAPTER THIRTY-ONE

The trip to our next destination seemed to take much longer than I had anticipated. When we left, my goal seemed clear, but somewhere along the way my focus faded, revealing something bigger ... my true purpose.

When we arrived at our altered destination, I found I was neither tired nor sore. Energy coursed through my body, though my mind felt a bit fogged. Something itched in the back of my memories, as if something were wrong, but I couldn't remember what. I knew out of instinct that Hollow could transport me great distances. It was an ability of the Horsemen and one that saturated me with power. If something was amiss, I could not imagine what it was. I had purpose. My destiny was at hand and our destination had turned out far better than I expected.

"I'm no expert," Quack observed from Hollow's saddle in front of me. "But this does not look like London."

I didn't recognize the coastal landscape below us either ... but somehow, I knew right where we were. An early morning chill filled the air, especially on the mountain top where we stood. Dawn had cracked the horizon. Residents stirred in the city below, oblivious to the fact that these moments would be their last.

"London is not where we were meant to go," I said out loud to Quack. "This is the very cradle of creation. A fitting place to begin our righteous crusade to cleanse humanity don't you think?"

Quack craned his neck around to peer at me with his little duck eyes. "Say what now?"

"We will bring about destruction to the African continent the way War, Famine and Pestilence have wrought destruction upon their continents. This is our corner of the world to conquer, and we shall scour it clean of humanity's filth."

"Was this a part of the original plan? I feel like I would remember this."

"My purpose has been laid out before me. I know what I've been called to do." I raised my sickle high into the air, holding it over my head, drawing power into my mantle. Familiar clouds began to gather overhead, unnatural and dark—full of fire rather than rain.

"Wow. That's a neat trick. How did you do that?" Quack raised a wing and his eyes turned a fiery orange, then a small angry cloud appeared over his head. "Woah, I could get into this. Maybe we could scour a little filth. Just the ones who pollute lakes and drink alcoholic seltzers."

"No more will this landscape bear the blight of mankind." I continued, swirling my sickle overhead, building the firestorm and watching it spread. "Cape Town South Africa will be the epicenter, but we will march up through the continent, delivering the very fires of Hell in our wake."

I brought my sickle down hard and with it came the storm, enveloping not only the city but the entire horn of the continent in Hellfire. Quack followed my gesture bringing down a gout of fire of his own, singeing the ground at our feet, causing Hollow to stamp his hooves irritably. A single feather fell along with it, smoldering red as it floated to the earth.

"Part of me knows you sound like a lunatic right now, but another part feels like you make a lot of sense." Quack stared at his smoldering feather as it fell to the ground beneath his miniature firestorm cloud. "That part is currently drunk with power, so we will be telling the rational half to shut up until we feel things out with this whole world domination plan."

I grinned at Quack's compliance and turned Hollow to begin our march to the north. Screams and shouts of panic rose from the city below, even over the roar of the flames. This was just the beginning. Soon the screams of an entire continent would be heard around the world.

As we began to move, the storm front moved with us, spreading coast to coast, allowing nothing to escape its hellish wrath.

"Come meet me, my brothers. Meet me, and our time on this planet will truly begin. We will render the Earth to ash and make way for new life, different life. It is time to start anew, absent the blight of humanity and all who infect it."

CHAPTER THIRTY-TWO

I slowed Hollow to a walk more for my sake than his. We paced along behind the impossible storm, basking in the wake of its utter destruction. Nothing survived. Not a tree, a bush, a bird, or berry. No humans or animals, no buildings or bridges. Everything was razed to ash and rubble, and we three, Quack, Hollow and me, were all who remained to witness it.

We had moved at a pace that seemed impossible to maintain. When we advanced, the world turned to a blur. We disappeared into the fire and smoke and together, became one force moving inexorably across the continent, like a hurricane sweeping the countryside with flame. The exercise was exhausting. As if I carried the storm on my shoulders and pushed it along with my withering feet. The burden weighed on me with every step and I could not understand why. This was the way of things. I was the bringer of death. The deliverer of fire and destruction. Why should this task weigh on me as if it were—

Before my mind came to a conclusion, Quack swooped out of the sky and landed on Hollow's head. The half dead horse objected with a huff and a whinny but didn't thrash or try to throw him off. Quack kept his wings outstretched and his head turned to the sky like some sort of crazy wizard on his tower, commanding his spells to rain down upon the landscape below.

"I return, oh great master of fire and flame."

"I told you to stop calling me that."

"But 'tis what you are, Master. The orchestrator of this great marvel."

Quack's words brought forth deep pangs of guilt and misery, and I was again left to wonder where they came from.

"I helped of course, lending my great power to yours."

"Your power?"

Quack put his wings down and looked at me.

"Yeah. You don't think you did all of this on your own, do you? I've been up there for hours fanning the storm."

"That was you?" I eyed him with no small amount of skepticism.

"I don't think I like your tone." Quack narrowed his eyes. "I fly around, winging life into this campfire of yours and this is the thanks I get?"

I let out a snort of laughter. "I stand corrected. Thank you for your help. I couldn't have done it without you."

"That's better." He paused staring at me for a moment. "Wait, was that sarcasm?"

"Nope. Hey, when you're flying around do you feel, I don't know..." Something inside fought against saying the words out loud. "Sort of guilty for what we're doing."

"Guilty?" Quack scoffed. "What else would we do? This is what we are. We are Death. We have always been and always will be Death. Would you rather be one of these creatures lying in our path? A human or some pathetic animal? Have you seen the ducks? They're the worst. Waddling their fat bodies around on spindly little legs. They look ridiculous. If I were a duck, I would throw myself into the firestorm out of sheer self-pity."

I nodded. "Ducks are a bit of a natural disaster. I'm sure they had their redeeming qualities though."

"Whatever. I'm flying up to stoke the flames again. You should think about helping me out whenever you're done with your little break here."

"Yes, sir." I shot him a salute and he flew off leaving me to my thoughts again. I knew I should do as Quack said and charge the storm forward, but I wanted to tease out this nagging feeling a little more.

"Your partner is correct you know." The new voice came from behind me, something that should have been impossible. My flames destroyed everything in their path. No one could be here, yet ...

I turned in my saddle to see a woman with shocking white hair and a black peacoat. She strolled in behind me, her boots raising little clouds in the ash as she walked. The woman wore a knowing smile that I found incredibly irritating. Something told me I knew this person. That I didn't like or should not trust her, but for the life of me I didn't remember why.

"You embraced your power with extraordinary ferocity." She hurried her steps to walk along side of me, but I noticed she stayed out of striking distance from my sickle. "You are doing your mantle proud. This ..." She gestured at the gigantic wall of smoke and fire billowing ahead of us. "Is far more impressive than anything even I could imagine."

Her grin, her words, her accolades, everything about this woman rubbed me wrong. That little voice inside me screamed louder than ever, bringing my conflict within to a head.

"What do you want? You have no place here."

The woman held up her hands in a sign of surrender and peace.

"I wish you no ill will. On the contrary, I want only for you to succeed. Your exploits will bring in a new age and I will, well —let's just say I have a personal stake in your success as well."

"What sort of stake?" I ground my teeth and kept one eye on her as she paced along beside me. "I don't like surprises."

She shrugged and maintained her knowing grin. "It's nothing for you to be concerned about. It has no bearing on your task at hand. And let me say you have done a stunning job as Death. Part of me never thought you would turn, but then—this."

She waved her hands ahead of us again.

"What do you mean turn? Turn from what?"

The voice inside me fought for control and I put my free hand to my head, wincing at the conflict in my mind. I'd been right. This woman, whoever she was, spelled nothing but trouble. I could not allow her to distract me. She would not dissuade me from my task.

Without another word I raised my hand and with a small effort of will, produced a fireball the size of a tank.

I hurled it at the stranger, but before it struck home, the woman exploded into a flock of pigeons, avoiding the blast. I could hear her voice cackling on the wind, but she did not return. The birds flew off toward the waste of dust and ash.

The voice inside me calmed the moment she was gone, but it did not abate completely. I'd had enough internal conflict at any rate. I would forge ahead and baptize my conflict within the firestorm and there my purpose would solidify. One purpose, one reason, one will.

I was about to charge forward when another stranger emerged out of nowhere. This time she came from the direction of the fire and flame. My eyes widened at the impossibility as the blue-haired woman walked straight toward me. She did not grin like my first visitor. Instead, she had a look of sheer determination. Even more strange was that internal voice. It seemed to cheer at the mere sight of this new interloper.

One thing was for sure, my internal conflict fought more than ever to stomp out any doubt as to my purpose. I dismounted and stepped forward in front of Hollow, holding my sickle aloft. Still, she came, looking more resolute than ever. When she was within ten paces, I raised my hand as before and unleashed a stream of fire no living being could withstand. This was not a single ball of flame, but a gout of fire, streaming from my hand like molten death.

I squinted my eyes at the blazing light, and when I was sure there would be nothing left but ash, I drew back my will to see she had disappeared. My inferno had reduced her to a pile no more recognizable than the other debris in which we stood.

The voice within me screamed with sorrow but it was weak now—beaten. Good. Now I could continue with the task at hand.

I turned, ready to climb into my saddle, but a hand gripped my shoulder from behind and jerked me around.

"Fire was sort of my thing first." It was the blue-haired woman. She had survived and without a single singed hair on her peacock-colored head. "You'll need to do better than that."

She slammed her hand into my chest before I had a chance to react. The blow was not hard, but it contained all the force of a speeding bus. I could not move, I could not breathe, I could however, begin to think.

"Come back to me you big dumb oaf."

Alex was her name. And I was not Death. I was Gabe, Gabriel Gantry.

"Come back to me or so help me I'll slap this thing out of your head so hard your ears will touch."

CHAPTER THIRTY-THREE

I coughed and tried to pull away, but Alex swept my feet and threw me to the ground. Her hand, and whatever was in it, never left my chest. For several long seconds I felt something within tear at my mind, fighting for dominance, but it was no use. It was ripped away like an angry cat and cast into the darkness. Not quite gone, but no longer in control.

"Ouch. Did you have to hit me that hard?"

"Welcome back there, big boy." Alex sat astride me, still holding her hand to my chest as if she were performing some sort of makeshift CPR.

I looked down without trying to move her away and saw the sturdy chain attached to my locket playing out between her fingers.

"Apparently you misplaced this when you gave me the sword yesterday." She pulled her hand away from my chest, keeping a wary eye on my face, no doubt looking for any sign that I was losing myself again.

"You wrapped it in with the sword. If I hadn't looked inside before I hid it, I would have never known."

A protective instinct in my brain kicked in and I tried to sit up to look at her. "Why did you unwrap the sword? What if it lured you in or entranced you somehow? You were only supposed to hide it. Don't play around with that thing."

She raised an eyebrow and I regretted my lecture immediately. Considering the glass house I had erected out of flame and destruction, I was in no position to throw stones.

"Sorry, I just want you to be safe."

Alex rolled off me and I stood with her. She wasted no time looping the locket around my head to let it rest against my chest. It felt both at home and somehow intrusive to my spirit. Like a weight against my chest that didn't quite allow me to breathe.

I laid my hand against it, thankful for its protection.

"Look out, I'm coming in hot."

I glanced up to see Quack—not quite flying. More like falling.

He tumbled through the air, headed straight for me and I had no choice but to catch him like a Hail Mary on Super Bowl Sunday. He hit my arms then thrashed in a flurry of feathers to right his overturned body and bring himself to a head-up position again.

"What the heck is going on? One second we're headed off to fight this Simeon guy, the next I'm flapping through the worst wildfire in the history of the earth. I can't believe I have any feathers left. Please tell me I didn't have anything to do with that. I haven't smoked in years. Cigarettes kill you know."

"I don't mean to be a spoilsport." Alex glanced toward the still raging firestorm to the North of us. "But is there a switch or something you can flip to turn this thing off?"

My brain had been so fogged I had forgotten about the firestorm. My mind felt fractured about many of the details over the last day or so. I turned to the storm and realized I had no idea how to flip the switch at all. Guilt rose into my chest like a lead-filled balloon. How did I produce something so large, so devastating? How far did this storm reach?

The answer was locked deep in that other consciousness. I took in a shocked breath as I realized my fires spanned the entire continent.

I had to stop this thing. I focused all my will and raised my sickle over my head. The storm continued to roil and rage, but then, after a moment, the smoke clouds began to break apart, the fire dimmed, and the sky peeked through. Within minutes the storm abated, leaving a scorched line across the landscape as far as the eye could see. Much of what we stood upon was desert but everything behind us was blackened ash. In front of us there was life. The promise of prosperity and untouched humanity.

Alex put a hand on my shoulder as I looked out at the unmolested landscape where my firestorm had not yet decimated all life.

"How many?" Tears filled my eyes as spotted memories and fractured thoughts came back to me. "Where are we and how many people died?"

"Gabe." Alex's voice sounded tender and full of empathy. "That was not you. The mantle did this. It was Death. You had no control. You were only along for the ride. You couldn't stop it."

"How many did I kill?" I shouted the words this time, my voice cracking as tears streamed down my face.

Alex paused and cast her eyes to the ground. "The population of South Africa, portions of Namibia and Botswana, which is where we are now, numbered just over sixty-two million."

The breath left my lungs in a rush as I snapped my head toward Alex to look at her for confirmation. She did not meet my eyes. My hands shook and my legs felt weak. I turned away then took three steps before falling to my knees to throw up in the ash covered sand.

I stayed like that for several minutes. Hovering on my hands and knees. Judas had been right. How would I ever atone for something like this? I had not hurt a few people; I had killed sixty million. My arrogant belief that I could control the mantle caused all of this. It was my fault.

To my surprise it was not Alex's voice that came to me first, but Quack's.

"I'm sorry."

It wasn't what he said but how he said it that made me straighten and look down at him. It wasn't meant as an empathetic statement, but rather a profession of guilt and sorrow.

"What do you have to be sorry for?" I kept the thought in my head instead of speaking it aloud. "You didn't do any of this, I did."

Quack waddled over to where I knelt on the ground. "You and I are joined. What you do I do. I could have been your voice of reason. I could have stopped you or at least tried, but I flew into the air like a crazy chicken hawk trying to rain destruction upon the earth. I love the earth, even if I do complain about all you ugly, pink, land sniffers. I did this too. I just want you to know, I'm sorry."

Quack laid his head on my knee, and I could not help but let out a chuckle among my sobs. Here was a duck, practically sitting in my lap apologizing for laying waste to all of South Africa. Annoying as he was, I could not ask for a better companion.

"Neither of you did this." Alex walked to the two of us huddled on the ground. She crouched next to me and stroked Quack's feathery head a few times. "You were not in control. The mantle took over and did what it was programmed to do. That's all. It's a horrible tragedy ... unthinkable, but you don't have the luxury of dwelling on it right now."

Alex's voice started off sounding soft and understanding but grew into something firm and commanding.

"The two of you still have a job to do."

She reached over, grabbed my wrist and forced my hand over to where the sickle lay in the ash.

"Sixty million is only a fraction of the people who will die if you don't stand up right now. You have to face Simeon and stop him. You can't let this setback get in your way."

"Setback." I jerked my hand out of her grasp. "Sixty million people is not a setback."

Alex gripped my wrist again and forced it down again. "Yes, it is when you're talking about eight billion here on Earth. Is that what you want on your conscience? Eight billion people dead because you refused to do anything about it? Because you were afraid to do anything?"

I glared at her for several long moments, but I knew she was right. No matter what had happened, I had to push this guilt down and fight. Fight with everything I had. The kid gloves were off. This was for keeps. Simeon would come at me with the full force of his mantle, and I would have to do the same.

I gathered my feet and stood, hefting my sickle at my side. "Thank you. I needed that."

Alex stood, then pulled my head toward her to kiss me full on the lips before I had a chance to pull away. There was a moment of sheer panic as I wondered whether my touch would kill her, but there seemed to be no ill effects.

"I already touched you once remember," she said. "Besides, I am dead. You can't kill me twice."

I laughed. "You're crazy."

"I know." She winked. "We should head out, though. I'm betting every military satellite in the world is zeroing in on us now that your fires have died out. I don't want to be here when they land half a dozen tactical missiles in our backyard. Could you give me a ride to my splice point before you get on with your business? Just make sure you keep that little trinket strapped to your neck."

I put my hand to the locket and nodded. "I promise. Come on, Quack. We have some Horseman ass to kick, and I can't do it without you."

Quack waddled in behind us and flapped his wings. "All right but I'm not sure I'll be able to produce anything like that firestorm again. That really took it out of me. Maybe a little one. We'll see."

I laughed as I pulled Hollow around and slid into the saddle. I hauled Alex up behind me and Quack fluttered in front, then Hollow took off at a gallop toward Alex's splice point.

"I'll take whatever you've got buddy. As long as we're in it together."

CHAPTER THIRTY-FOUR

"So, you're telling me I didn't do any of that?"

Quack and I rode into one of the most iconic locations in all of Paris. The Louvre not only housed some of the most fantastic and priceless works of art in the world, it also had a stunning open courtyard connected to the Tuileries Gardens, a fifty-five-acre park allowing easy access for thousands of eager tourists or perhaps a horde of Snot Zombies looking for a fight. The sun hadn't even made it over the horizon yet, so the usual droves had yet to arrive. I just hoped we could get on with our business before the general public got involved.

"I'm sure you did something." I didn't know whether I was making Quack feel better because he didn't have a hand in our earlier destruction of South Africa or worse because his powers weren't exactly … apocalyptic in scale.

"I thought I was helping," he said, as we rode into the courtyard of the Louvre. "Why else would I be flying around in that firestorm shouting like a lunatic."

I chuckled, biting off a retort. "Speaking of flying around. Why don't you get airborne? I want you to be my eye in the sky in case Simeon has any surprises in store. Let me know if he flanks my blindside with a bunch of zombies or something."

Quack lifted a wing in salute. "Will do."

I got ready to throw him into the air, but he stopped me, turning to meet my eyes.

"Hey. Be careful, all right. I don't want to have to fish you out of those gnashing pools again."

I nodded. "I promise. And thanks for looking out for me."

I boosted him into the air and he took off, flapping his wings to gain altitude. I watched him until he was nothing more than a dot in the sky, then I heard a voice coming from the direction of the Gardens.

"Well, well." Simeon rode up on his gleaming white stallion looking relaxed and stylish as always. He still wore his top hat, glasses and trench coat, but now I noticed he had a civil war style rapier lashed to the side of his saddle. An odd accoutrement for Pestilence. I wondered why he would have such a thing, unless …

"That is quite a wardrobe change." Simeon grinned. "The cloak looks a bit tedious, but your horse is very intimidating. What happened to the rest of him? Get eaten by a pack of wolves?"

I glanced down at Hollow's half exposed skull. "Just a little eczema. I have some cream on order. He'll be fine."

Simeon let out a laugh. "I'm sure. I have to say, when I sensed a fellow Horseman here in my territory, I hardly expected to find you."

I spread my arms. Making a show of displaying my large deadly looking sickle. "I heard you were throwing a party and I wanted to see what all the fuss was about."

Simeon never lost his smile. "Oh, we have quite a party." As he spoke, droves of Snot Zombies began to jerk and shamble out of the trees and shrubbery behind him, filling the park with his hordes. All at once I ceased worrying about any tourists who might wander into our little discussion. Most of them, along with much of the population of Paris, were probably infected with Simeon's nanites. Any wayward tourists who could have been hurt were already here.

"You're welcome to join our little soirée, but I doubt that's what you're here for."

I smiled back at him. "No, I have a party of my own. But I don't think the guests will mingle well."

Simeon made a show of looking behind me. I had my back to the empty courtyard and museum while he had his back to acres of open ground full of sniffling zombies. "I think your guests are a little late."

"Fashionably, but they always arrive when I call. I just wanted to give you a chance to give this up. Call me a softy, but I don't want to fight if we don't have to. There's no reason to kill millions of people. Put down your mantle. I can help if you don't feel you can do it on your own. Let's stop this madness. You were … are human. There must be some part of you that believes in preserving your own people."

Simeon lost a bit of his mirth at that and nodded. "I do think about that sometimes. About the end of all mankind."

"We can prevent that from happening. You and I. Right now. Just lay down your mantle and set these people free."

Simeon nodded and for a moment I thought he might actually do it. But then he reached down and drew his rapier out of its sheath and glared at me with villainous eyes.

"I think about the end of mankind and cheer. And when I'm done here, I will ride down to The Nine and rule all those I have sent to their end."

"Oh, I think you might be biting off a little more demon than you can chew with that one."

Simeon didn't care. He simply heeled his horse and charged straight toward me. I made no attempt to move but rather took a more defensive stance as he struck at me with his rapier.

I parried his blow as he galloped past and turned to meet his next attack, but he smiled and pointed his blade behind me instead. I had fallen for his trick. I had turned my back on his snot laden troops. Lucky for me my reinforcements were close at hand.

Unlike his zombies, wraiths didn't need doors, windows or even open ground to advance. They just rushed through the walls, floor and ceilings of the Louvre and streaked toward Simeon's horde. While he had no doubt instructed his troops to tear me apart, I had simply ordered mine to keep his Zombies occupied. They would fight, block and bar their advance but would not harm any of the hapless participants in Simeon's crusade.

Simeon saw his horde enveloped and overwhelmed in seconds and screamed in frustration. He ordered more and more of his Snot Zombies into the fight, but Paris had no shortage of the dead. I could raise far more than he could call, even if he turned every human on the continent.

"It's over Simeon. You can't beat me. Your minions are no match for my wraiths. They are a parlor trick. Human tech. They can't stand against a true Horseman's power. Give up and I'll let you live."

Simeon let out a guttural scream and charged again, rapier high in the air. He struck down hard and I parried again with my sickle. He managed to stay close this time which put me at a disadvantage. My sickle was six feet long making his rapier far more suited to our close quarters fight. Something Simeon obviously knew.

He struck at me again and again, never allowing me to retreat out of his strike range. I could barely repel his attack and it would not be long before he would get one of his strikes past my defenses.

It occurred to me that any wound inflicted on me should heal if his rapier were a Topside weapon. Simeon would know this as well, however. He would have planned for it. Either his sword was a special delivery from nether-parts unknown or my new Horseman health plan had holes in it I didn't know about. Either way, this fight was rapidly devolving into a losing battle. If I didn't do something quick, Simeon would win after all.

I parried another strike and lashed out with a strike of my own, but I was thrown off balance. My sickle arced wide. I had no way to avoid Simeon's next swing, so I rolled out of my saddle and onto the ground. I had one last trick up my sleeve, but I didn't want to use it. I had no idea if I could control my firestorm powers, but I had to try.

I lashed out with my arm and gathered my will as Simeon reared his mount around for a killing blow. The dark part of my consciousness thrashed against its bonds, but I focused and forced my power in his direction. A huge fireball emitted from my palm, streaking toward his body. Simeon was forced to dismount or be decimated as well.

Hollow charged Simeon's mount, rearing back and attacking with his front hooves, forcing the other horse out of the way. With no cover, Simeon was defenseless. I held out a hand ready to incinerate him with another blast but held back.

"Last chance," I said. "Lay down your mantle or I will take it from you."

Simeon's wild eyes shot everywhere, seeking escape or an avenue for attack. Then his shoulders relaxed and he straightened. He splayed his arms wide in a display of surrender and smiled at me.

"I guess you win," he said. "Come claim your prize."

I did not move as he still held his rapier, but I could not destroy him either. He had surrendered. Incinerating him now would be like killing an unarmed man.

Quack's frantic voice broke into my mind, disrupting the momentary conundrum.

"Look out, Gabe. You have company coming from the East."

"East? Which way is East?"

"Your right."

I barely had time to turn my head before I was swarmed by a mass of insects so large it nearly knocked me off my feet. I tried to turn my pyrotechnics against the oncoming wave, but it was too much. Insects clouded my vision, crawled into my mouth and nose and into my ears. They weighed me down until I could no longer stand or even hold my sickle. It crashed to the ground with a clang, and I fell to my knees as more insects piled on, suffocating, stinging, biting. It was unbearable and overwhelming. I was defeated before I had a chance to swing. Just like that, Simeon had won … or rather, Jake.

Famine had joined the battle. I had been so distracted with Simeon I had not sensed his counterpart. Against two Horsemen I had no chance.

I waited for the killing blow to come—for Simeon's rapier to lance the layers of insects and pierce my heart but he had something far worse in mind.

The insects parted from my ears and eyes allowing me to see and hear, if only for a moment. Simeon came into view, leaning over me in grinning triumph. Jake stood behind him, not grinning but stone-faced and serious in the grip of his power.

"I guess I should have told you Jake and I met earlier and discussed this little reunion. You see, an angel came and told us you might stop by for a visit and suggested we join forces."

To my horror I felt some of the weight peel away from my chest and then a yank at my neck.

"She also told me about this little trinket you carry. She said I should keep it safe for you." He winked at me as he let the locket swing over my head then dropped it into a thick leather pouch, careful not to touch it. He secured the top, tying it with a long leather thong to be sure it could not fall out then waved it before me again. I tried to scream but Jake's insects choked off the sound.

"Don't worry. We aren't going to hurt you. We just want you to finish what you started down there in Africa. Without this little keepsake of yours, I think you'll head right back down there and pick up where you left off."

He grinned at me again.

"You take care of yourself. I have a feeling the next time we meet, you and I, we'll be the best of friends."

Simeon waved then turned to Jake. "Wrap him up and keep him busy until we leave. I don't want him tailing us out of here. After that, have your bugs go their own way."

Jake nodded and his insects clogged my senses again, leaving me in the dark. Helpless and defenseless against the mantle waiting to turn me into the monster I was destined to become.

CHAPTER THIRTY-FIVE

Once the mummifying insects dispersed and allowed me to move again, I was free to do anything I pleased. I'm sure there were many courses of action I could have taken. I just chose not to take them. If I didn't call on the power of the mantle, at least I'd stay myself. Instead, I ambled to the outskirts of town and looked for the dirtiest dive bar I could find. I went inside, Death cloak, duck and all, ordered an American Bourbon, sent Alex a message to let her know about my epic failure, and settled in for a good old-fashioned bender.

The bar made me feel right at home. If there were a universal language it would be written in the dive bar. Graffiti covered the walls, the chairs and stools were mismatched, the place smelled like the wrong side of a fat man's t-shirt and the beer was served in plastic cups. The only problem was the *actual* language barrier. The bartender served me the triple-shot of juice, but he was pointing at my feathered companion perched on the stool next to me, rapid firing an angry stream of French dialogue and gesturing like Quack had pooped on his bar.

I looked over to make sure Quack had not done just that, then looked back at the bartender and smiled.

"He's my therapy duck," I raised my voice, annunciating every word. I never understood why Americans thought doing this would make them easier to understand, but as soon as I was faced with a language barrier, I found myself doing the exact same thing.

"I'm allergic to dogs, see." I shouted extra slow. "So, they gave me a duck. He's really quite annoying once you get to know him."

The man auctioneered another stream of French at me, then waved his hands in a dismissive gesture and walked away, apparently disgusted with either my communication skills or my choice of companion.

"Thank you," I said as he walked away. "I like your pants too."

I took a sip of my bourbon, then gulped half of it down, wincing at the burn.

"You think he has any crackers back there," Quack said. "Or even some stale bread. All that flying and burning and catastrophic destruction really took it out of me."

"I don't think he has much in the way of hors d'oeuvres. If we weren't in such a dive, he'd probably call the cops … unless they're all Snot Zombies too."

"What do you expect?" Quack let out a little laugh. "You're carrying around a sickle that's taller than you. I'm surprised everyone hasn't called the cops. And don't even get me started about your horse."

I laughed.

"Maybe the Grim Reaper is sort of a regular thing in France. They probably think we're off to some early morning costume party."

Quack honked out an audible laugh of his own. "That guy has no sense of humor. The Grim Reaper and a duck walk into a bar together and he doesn't even take a swing at a punch line."

I downed the rest of my drink and slammed the glass onto the bar, drawing a disdainful glare from the barkeep. "Keep 'em coming Pierre. I want to be good and inebriated fifteen minutes from now and that's not going to happen with you wee, weeing the customers down there."

I got ready to slide my glass down the bar in an even further belligerent display of assery when a hand fell on my arm to stop me.

"Have you lost your mind?"

Alex stood next to me, her grip locked so tight around my forearm it hurt.

"Uh-oh." Quack eyed Alex then nodded at me. "I think we might be in trouble."

"Yeah. You got that right." She turned her attention to Quack and he ruffled his feathers in a nervous attempt to back away. "You're supposed to keep him from doing anything stupid. Some Jiminy Cricket you turned out to be."

Quack cleared his throat. "Easy on the cricket talk. The big guy is a little bug shy right now."

"Is that right." She turned her attention back to me, in no way showing understanding or sympathy. If she had a big plastic cockroach in her pocket, I was pretty sure she would put it right on my head.

"Feeling a little sorry for ourselves, are we? Thought you would head in, tails between your legs and tie one on while the rest of the world suffered and died. Seems like a reasonable thing to do, especially when you're the only being on earth able to stop it from happening."

She glared at me for a minute then threw her hand off my arm and tsked with disgust.

"I'm getting a little tired of having to come up here and pull you together. What happened to the guy who faced down demons just to save his friend's bar?"

"There was only one demon, not two, and he didn't sneak up on me when I wasn't looking and fill my mouth with spiders."

"You're such a baby," Alex said. "So what if Jake got the drop on you. You're here now, ready to fight again. Make them pay for—"

"They got the locket."

That stopped her in her tracks.

"I know."

I looked up and stared at her in stunned silence for a moment.

"Don't look so surprised," she said. "You wouldn't have messaged me for some little setback. I figured it was big, and nothing could be bigger than that."

I nodded. "How did I get such a smart partner?"

"You didn't set the bar all that high." She smiled. "Did Sammy tip them off? Once I was back in The Nine, I had a chance to think about it a little more and figured she might let Simeon know, but it was too late to warn you. I did go talk to Judas though."

"What?" I didn't think it was possible to be any more surprised, but Alex kept pulling rabbits out of her hat. "I'll bet he was happy to hear about our little mutiny."

"He's a scary guy when he gets angry."

I nodded. "Wait till he brings up the llamas."

Alex screwed up her face in confusion but ignored my comment. "He was pretty mad at first, but when I told him the coin transformed into the mantle he calmed down and saw things the same way we did."

"Wow. I can't believe you got him to listen long enough to hear about the coin."

"It wasn't easy. He unleashed Mastema and everything, but he saw reason in the end. We talked about the locket and the possibility of losing it. Bad as it is, he said you should still be able to resist the call of the mantle as long as you resist the urge to use your power."

I rolled my eyes. "No problem. I can just hide in here and shoot spit wads at them."

"That's not what I meant." Alex scowled. "He said don't travel, for one. You're in the realm of the Horsemen and most susceptible to falling to its power when you do that."

"Well, that explains what happened last time."

Alex nodded. "That trip across the globe was enough to pull you in. You should be able to make a few short trips to catch up to Simeon and Jake though."

I shook my head. "And do what? I can't separate them from their mantles without the locket. Even if I manage to beat them it won't do any good."

Alex looked down and I knew she had more to say but didn't want to say it.

"Judas told you something else, didn't he? He knows another way." It was a statement, not a question.

Alex offered a reluctant nod. "Judas said you do not fall under the same rules as a Niner anymore. You have several advantages, but there is also one big disadvantage."

She paused and lowered her head. I reached out to pull her chin up so her eyes would meet mine. "What is it?"

"You can die." It was almost a whisper. "Not like we die, but different. He is not sure what happens to your soul, but he knows you would be gone forever. If that happens, your mantle is left behind."

I let the possibilities play through my mind. "So, if I kill the Horsemen, they will lose their mantles but if they kill me, my mantle just reverts back to the coin and they get nothing." I chuckled. "That's brilliant."

Alex punched me in the arm. "It is not brilliant. You could die. You could change. There are lots of things that could go wrong."

"Yes." I nodded. "But you said it yourself. I am the only one who can stop them. If I don't lay it all on the line who else will?

I have to try. I will resist the urge to turn. Quack." I spun and faced my feathered companion. "This is your job. It's important. You must keep me from turning. You have to resist it too. Don't wait for a sign. Keep reminding me to keep my head straight. Can you do that?"

Quack raised a wing in salute. "As long as we're within communication distance, I'll be a constant irritation in that big, blubbery brain."

I laughed. "Not all that unusual, but thank you."

"You're entrusting your eternal fate to a duck? Unbelievable."

I turned back to Alex and saw the frustration and worry in her face. I searched my mind for the right words then gave up and kissed her instead. She resisted at first, then wrapped her hands around my neck and held me tight and I held her too. When we broke our embrace, I smiled and stared into her eyes. "Thank you. You're always here when I need you."

"I always will be," she said. "That's a promise. Now go get those wannabes before I change my mind and sit here and drink with you."

I nodded and reached to the floor where my sickle lay on the ground. As soon as I picked it up, the bartender started in with his French barrage and hand gestures again.

"This guy keeps talking about my pants." I shrugged and whispered to Alex. Then I pointed to the bottom of my frayed looking cloak. "Joke's on you buddy. I'm not wearing any."

The bartender stopped his barrage for a moment looking perplexed, then continued faster than ever, motioning to the giant weapon I held in my hand.

"Guess I better go," I said.

Alex nodded then reached into her pocket and offered me something before I could leave.

"I almost forgot. Terayn said to take these."

She revealed a pair of familiar looking white tablets. She had provided them on another occasion, and they were a wonder cure for a hellish hangover. Apparently, they were good for focus and fighting off an alter ego as well.

I popped the pills into my mouth and dry swallowed them.

"Thanks. And don't worry. It'll take more than a couple of losers on horseback to bring me down."

Alex nodded. "Be sure it does. If there's anything I can do from the rooftops you let me know."

I nodded. Then turned to head out to my showdown with the two most powerful gunslingers the planet has ever known.

CHAPTER THIRTY-SIX

Saying my confrontation with Simeon and Jake would be complicated was like saying quantum loop gravity was a little challenging. First there was the obvious. It was two against one. They hadn't moved out of the region and I could sense that they were still together, probably anticipating another counter attack. At least I wouldn't have to go far to find them. Second, I could not use my powers. Not much, anyway. I used the Horseman's mantle to travel a few short miles and I could already feel the allure of its call. It was like a drug to an addict. I wanted to resist, but something inside me said I could just try a little and it would be okay. Then maybe a little more—and then more, until I didn't care about the little taste and just upended the whole bottle. The temptation made me want to itch and twitch all over and I had to actively grind my teeth at times just to resist.

As much as I was at a disadvantage, I did not roll into this nuthouse without a rubber chicken up my sleeve. I could sense where they were headed. I knew where they would be. I had a plan.

I waited for them at the end of an abandoned street. Simeon and Jake looked all around and I could tell they sensed me, but it took a moment for them to realize where I was. After all, I chose a rather unorthodox form of transport for one of the four Horsemen of the apocalypse. They looked at me, squinted, shielded their eyes and squinted some more. Jake even pointed at me, trotted in my direction then stopped within shouting distance, leaving the bug infested snot zombie horde behind.

"A Smart car?" Simeon laughed out loud. "I must admit I expected you to try some sort of half-witted attack, but I did not expect this. Please, get out. You're embarrassing us all. What would the general population think if they saw Death buzzing around in a bright yellow roller skate?"

"I feel dirty." Quack sat in the cramped seat next to me, sulking with his head low and his feathers ruffled. "Why is The Grim Reaper and his fearsome companion rolling to battle in a matchbox. This isn't even a real car. We could have at least found a Camaro."

"Hush. We need a car to make my plan work and I don't know how to hot wire a car. This one had the keys in the ignition."

"Great. I get stuck with the Horseman with no street skills."

I hunched forward and moved my knee so I could roll the miniature window down.

"Blow me!"

That was enough to bring both Jake and Simeon to rolling laughter.

"Can you just drop me off somewhere so I can pretend I'm not with you?"

I ignored Quack's commentary and waited for the laughter to calm almost all the way down. Then I slammed our clown car into drive and floored it toward their skittish mounts, blowing the Micky Mouse horn the whole way. It had the desired effect. Their horses reared, bringing any remaining laughter to a halt and forcing Jake and Simeon to wrestle their mounts back under control again.

I turned at the last second, flipping the car around like Mario Cart with less gusto, and put my plan into action. I floored the little Smart car and immediately wished there was another switch or pedal I could push to go faster. At this rate, Simeon and Jake would be on me in seconds—a geriatric with a walker had more acceleration. I just had to hope we had enough of a head start.

"Would it help if I got out and flapped?"

I didn't spare a glance at Quack even though at our speed, I had plenty of time to look around.

"If you had a better plan, you should have spit it out before the high-speed chase."

Quack turned his head and stared at me without saying anything.

"Okay high-speed is a stretch, but you should have said something either way. We're in it now, so strap in or get out."

Quack made no move to fasten his seatbelt, but I did see our target dead ahead and steered straight for the entrance. It was a three-story parking garage with a spiral drive. I hit the ramp without letting off the gas and squealed the tires all the way up. Somehow Simeon and Jake were still several seconds behind despite our lackluster getaway. I needed to make it to the top before they got inside. For my plan to work, I needed them to stop on each floor and search through the sea of parked cars to find me. If I announced my location before they got here, this would be a very short battle indeed.

I got to the rooftop. Slammed on the brakes and shut the hamster wheel down. Hollow waited patiently for me in the middle of the rooftop parking area. I was surprised at how much I had missed him. Given the alternative, who wouldn't.

"All right." I pulled Quack out of the car and tossed him into the air. "You know what to do."

"Anything, as long as I don't have to ride in that clown car anymore." Quack took flight and circled the building, diving down over the edge.

Even though I sensed them nearby, I had no way of knowing exactly where Simeon and Jake were without Quack's eyes. I needed him to be my lookout until they got here. I didn't have long to wait.

"They're on the first floor." Quack whispered into my mind. I wanted to tell him there was no need to whisper, but I figured what was the point? "You were right. They're poking around, looking for you. There are about a million smart cars in here. It might take a while."

I swung myself up into Hollow's saddle and peered out at the city skyline. "Just tell me when they move on to the second floor."

I held my breath, waiting, anticipating. Not just for the moment when I would strike, but my body knew it was going to get a taste. It was going to get a sample of the drug it longed for. The power for which it craved. That would be the true battle. I would have to hold it back. Resist before the taste became a full-on Reaper Runaway. I had to hold it at bay or Simeon would win without lifting a finger.

"There they go." Quack hammered into my thoughts. "They're riding up … They're in the spiral drive … Now they're on the second … Oh crap. I think they saw me. The one in the hat is pointing. Oh, no. Lots of bugs. Gotta go …"

"Quack!" I couldn't help but shout his name out loud. The second I did I realized I had just given myself away. In the silence of the uninhabited city my voice had been like a thunderclap.

I was out of time.

I gathered my will and concentrated my power to the floor beneath my feet, unleashing a storm of hellfire between the first and third floors. Flames burst out of the outer openings like a blast furnace, turning the parking garage into a kiln. I could feel the heat rise around the rooftop as it melted everything and everyone inside.

The power that coursed through my body was like sweet paradise. I closed my eyes and threw my head back, reveling in the sensation. It felt right. More than right, it felt like home. Every missing piece fell into place, every wrong made right. All except …

I took a breath and forced the power back down, realizing it was about to overtake me. I wrestled with every muscle, every fiber, every nerve that shouted for it to continue, but I fought it, nonetheless. After what felt like an eternity, Death's mantle lost its grip and I was able to reassert myself once again. I gasped as the fires ebbed below. It was almost too much. I had nearly passed the point of no return … but it had worked. Nothing could have survived that inferno. Not even me.

I nudged Hollow around and together we walked down the circle drive to the second floor. It was a ruin of melted cars and spalled concrete. The fire had rendered everything to slag. It was a miracle I had not brought the whole building down. I picked my way through the destruction, weaving through the melted husks of parked cars, then I saw them. Two lifeless lumps just to the left of the exit. They had almost made it out … almost.

They were all but unrecognizable. I could see the leather saddles, lying sideways on the ground, still strapped to the gruesome husks that used to be their horses. I regretted what these two beautiful animals had been attached to. The sight of them made me retch. I could not help but turn away, then I forced myself to look again. I would remember this moment. I would remember what it took to bring these Horsemen down along with all the innocent lives who paid the price for their arrogant lust for power … our lust for power. My hands were covered in that blood as well, mantle or no mantle, and that was something I might never come to terms with.

I stared at the gruesome husks for several long moments then something came into focus. A pouch, mangled and shriveled by the heat but still recognizable. It was looped around the horn of Simeon's saddle.

I kicked my leg over Hollow and dismounted to make my way over to the gruesome mass of flesh. If my locket was still inside, still retrievable, I needed to get it. Bring it back. I was still convinced it was important. An item of incredible power could not be left for just anyone to find.

My feet crunched on broken glass and crumbling concrete. The smell was all but unbearable, but I forced myself to move closer. It would only take a second. Then another sound made me jump. A screech as a door opened onto the stairwell just behind the dormant, steaming mass of flesh and leather. The protected stairwell. The one place in every building designed to resist a raging fire.

"You!" Simeon limped out of the door, followed close behind by Jake. Gone were his dark glasses and cool demeanor. His eyes bulged and he pumped his fists, panting with fury and rage. "Forget the Horsemen and your mantle. I'm going to tear you apart and throw pieces of your corpse out every window of this building."

CHAPTER THIRTY-SEVEN

Simeon did not even wait for one of my award-winning retorts. A bit rude considering his overly theatrical entrance. He charged straight at me, his rapier raised in the air, ready to strike.

He looked more than a little worse for wear. His perfect goatee was half singed away and his stylish trench coat smoldered in tatters. His face didn't appear much better. It was streaked black, and I wasn't sure if his flushed appearance was due to his fury or burns from the inferno. He still had his hat, however. Somehow it remained on his head, intact and flawless.

Jake's clothes were less flame touched and the expression he wore on his face differed from his companion's. He worked his hands in the telltale way that said he was calling upon his power, but I saw regret in his eyes. I recognized that sadness ... that desperation. He was in the grips of the mantle and had no way of pulling free. He no longer wanted to do its bidding, but he couldn't help it. The call was too strong, the addiction too powerful. His eyes were full of apology, but his actions were still full of death.

Simeon had no such qualms. I felt the sheer force of his

mantle burst out in a wave of energy that cracked several of the concrete support pillars around the structure. His horde would be back on the move with more determination than ever. Once they got here, the battle would be over.

I raised my sickle to block Simeon's first blow, parrying it off to the side, thankful he was not a swordsman. If he knew how to use his blade for anything other than a makeshift baseball bat, I would have been dead already. He swung his sword around again and again. I blocked his advance, but he was fast, and I was losing ground. Worse, they were both building power within their mantle and that was something I could not match. Insects began to pelt my face, distracting me from the fight. I thought Jake could have brought far more power to bear but perhaps he resisted the urge to go all out. I used a trickle of my own power to flash fry the nearby bugs but that brought the ravenous monster within me back to life. It shouted and screamed inside my head. Writhed and struggled to be set free. If only I would allow it to fulfill its destiny, my life would be complete. I would no longer be in danger.

More insects came and I had to fry them away too. I staggered away from Simeon as he swung his blade at me again. I could hear his Snot Zombies coming now. They were stumbling up the ramp, climbing the walls, ascending the stairwell. Soon I would be overrun.

I took a wild swing at Simeon, driving him back, but it was a fruitless effort. A pair of Snot Zombies grabbed me from behind. I reached for my power out of instinct. I burned them to ash in an instant but using that much power broke past the wall holding the mantle at bay. I staggered, dropping my sickle, clasping my head in my hands. It was too much. The mantle grew within me and this time it would not be denied.

I groaned in the darkness. I had lost. I could not win. My only choice was to let Simeon kill me and rob him of attaining the last mantle when my Sickle turned back into a coin. If only I could see his face when that happened.

"What are you waiting for?" I shouted at Simeon. "Kill me."

"Simeon seemed to sense the shift as well and held back his killing blow. He stared at me for a moment, confused by my sudden surrender, then his expression grew into a wide grin.

"I think not. Our brother approaches. I will wait for him to arrive and watch him destroy you instead."

He took several steps back, lowering his sword and widened his smile amidst his ruined goatee. "I'll tell you a little secret about the mantle of the Horsemen. If you embrace the power, it becomes a part of you. I am still Simeon, Jake is still Jake. But you ... you resist the power. Try to drive it out. In your case the mantle will shove you into the corner where you belong and take over. You will be nothing but a broken puppet. A witness to the mantle's will."

I grimaced, struggling to maintain control of my own mind. "You would know all about that, wouldn't you?"

I referred to the fact that he had done that same thing to poor Ryan Rokuda when he hijacked the body he now inhabited. Somewhere inside him Ryan still existed, scared and hidden, but alive. A prisoner within his own body while Simeon held the rudder. Now it seemed I was destined to suffer the same fate.

"I do know quite a bit about that." Simeon nodded. "And I will enjoy watching Death eat you up inside inch by inch."

He was right. Death was taking over. The mantle crept in, soaking my consciousness like an inevitable tide. I screamed and staggered, collapsing onto the ground. Simeon's zombies had stopped and so had Jake's bugs. Both apparently content to watch me go mad. It was over. Death had saturated my very existence. I had failed Alex and Judas. I had failed humanity. The mantle pulled me tight within its grasp. If Simeon didn't kill me now, Death would take over and ravage the Earth.

"Jake," I pushed myself up and reached out to him in desperation. "Kill me, please." I sucked in a breath. "Kill me so I can't do any more damage."

I fell, all but losing myself in the darkness. Then, through the shadows I felt something change. Not within me, but outside. Simeon felt it too for he stood bolt upright, turning his attention to somewhere on the horizon.

"No," he said. "But that's impossible."

I recognized the change. I had felt it before. It was a turn in the battle. A shift in the tide of war. I fought harder to resist the mantle, seeing a glimmer of hope in the darkness. I struggled to open my eyes and look around. Simeon's Snot Zombies had made their way to our floor, but they seemed somehow confused, conflicted. As if they weren't sure who, or what they were fighting for.

"Jake." It was all Simeon had time to say before War burst out of the entry ramp and charged them both.

Zoe. How could she have taken the mantle again after all we did to save her? She would be overwhelmed in moments and all four Horsemen would be back. Free to ravage the earth. I pushed myself up and struggled to get to my feet.

War rode in on her warhorse, broadsword raised high in the air and ready to strike, but Jake was already working at full power again. He lashed out with a swarm of insects, blinding her and throwing off her aim. She swung her massive ebony weapon but missed him by a mile.

The buzzing stinging insects caused her to thrash for a moment, but she spotted Simeon crouched to her right, several yards away. She turned her mount and charged. Simeon in turn brought his Snot Zombies to bear. War may have confused them for a moment but in the end, they were the minions of Pestilence and did his bidding. They piled in front of War's charge blocking her with sheer numbers. Simeon laughed as they pulled her to the ground and overwhelmed her with their weight.

"War is nothing without her armies, you of all people should know that." Simeon walked toward her while his Snot Zombies held her at bay. "A dictator without a country is nothing but a beggar on the street."

War hammered and slashed beneath the throng of sniffling bodies, but it was no use. Simeon was right. She had no real power here. Simeon controlled the population and without that, War had nothing.

It was up to me. I had to do something. Had to stop Simeon. There had to be a way. I could not let him have Zoe. Not after all she had been through. I stood and readied myself to unleash a torrent of power hoping it would kill Simeon before Death overtook me, then I remembered something. A way to win if I could just get to it.

I glanced over to where I saw the amulet tied to the ruined horse's saddle and my heart sank. Jake was already there. He worked the knot, pulling the pouch free. It was my last hope, and he had gotten to it first.

Simeon saw him as well and laughed. "Only a few steps and you could have been free. This was destined to happen. If it weren't, fate would have given you the locket and I would be the one lying on the ground groveling at your feet."

He turned his attention toward War, but I kept my eyes on Jake. He peered down at the pouch in his hand then at me. All at once the winds of fate changed. Jake tossed me the pouch with a sad but knowing smile. I caught it in the air and yanked the locket free before Simeon even knew what happened.

The moment the metal touched my skin I felt Death's mantle retreat from my consciousness. It left me free and fully myself once again, no trace of Death's will within me.

I took a single step forward and willed the heat around Simeon to rise. He froze in place, feeling the change he turned toward me. I smiled and showed him the locket. He jerked his head around to look at Jake who would not meet his eyes, then

Simeon turned his glare to me again, fury written all over his face.

He started to raise an arm to bring his power to bear but I raised the temperature around him a few more degrees, just enough to make his very existence all but unbearable.

"Send your snot monsters away, or we do a reenactment of the Salem Witch Trials right here."

Simeon thought about it for a moment, then his Snot Zombies began to retreat in the creepiest way possible. Like spiders walking in reverse in jerky unnatural motions. War rose from beneath a pile of Simeon's sniffling, sneezing henchmen and stood behind him.

"You too, Jake," I said. "No offense, but you might not be able to help yourself. I know how strong the call of the mantle is. Come over here and I don't want to hear so much as a mosquito buzz around my head."

Jake put his hands up and hurried over to stand next to Simeon.

"This is not over." Simeon chuckled. "You may kill me here, but I will be back and when I return from the Pools imagine what will happen when I tell the council about your little toy there. The dark master has been searching for that locket for an eternity. I'll bet he will be very interested in you and the fact that you have been lolling it around The Nine like it was your own."

All at once it came to me. I knew the purpose of the locket. What the origin artifact could do and its true power. The implication rocked me to my core.

"Release me and we can still ..."

I walked over to Simeon and thrust the locket against his face, stopping his villainous tongue before he said another word.

CHAPTER THIRTY-EIGHT

Simeon opened his mouth in a silent scream. I took no small satisfaction in his sudden surprise and frozen horror. I saw the defeat in his eyes. An expression of ultimate failure and I never looked away as his hat fell to the ground beside him. The crown given as his mantle. Not what I expected, though I supposed it made sense, in a strange modernistic sort of way.

I was even more surprised to see the ordeal was not over.

Simeon, as I mentioned earlier, was not really Simeon. He was a hijacker within an innocent's body. The locket not only had the power to separate the mantle from the user, but also Simeon's spirit from Ryan's body. I continued to watch as Simeon was torn away from his unnatural shell like an opaque undergarment, left to float, powerless to run or fight.

My mantle, the giant sickle, shrank in a flash of white light at the same time returning to its natural state as a silver denarius in my palm. The terror I saw written on Simeon's ethereal face was no longer a joy to watch. Even in his half existent state, Simeon realized what was about to happen. The coin began to draw at his midsection, pulling him in as he let out another silent scream. He reached for me, trying to grab onto my arms and shoulders but it was no use. His ghostly fingers found no purchase in the real world. The coin drew Simeon in, inch by pained distorted inch, until, with a flash of bright light, the venomous ex-Horseman was gone.

Ryan collapsed to the ground in a heap, leaving Jake, Zoe and myself to stare at the coin I held in my hand.

We all remained frozen in silence for a moment, then Jake looked at me in terror.

I shook my head before he said anything.

"That's not going to happen to you." I took a step toward him, but he matched me with a step back. "Maybe we should try this some other time. That locket may need to cool off or something."

Jake bumped into War as he took another step back. She had moved in behind while his eyes were fixed on the locket. It gave me just enough time to reach out and touch his arm with the warm metal surface.

He went rigid for a moment, but then he relaxed and the scale shaped charm he wore around his neck fell to the ground. We all held our breath for another heartbeat, but nothing else happened. Jake was still Jake, and his mantle was gone.

"Thank you," he said. "I never thought I would get rid of it. I am really sorry about all of this. I never meant for things to get this far. I just wanted a way to stay Topside, you know? I didn't want a bunch of power or for all those people to die. That Simeon guy. He was a lunatic. He would fit right in at the Judas Agency."

I nodded then something occurred to me.

"Wait. What did you do to Quack?"

Jake blinked.

"My duck. What did you do to my duck?" A mix of worry and anger rose inside of me as I thought of my companions last words about the overwhelming insects. If Jake had hurt him, or worse ... I might need my sickle after all.

Jake held up his hands seeing my growing fury. "He's okay. I just drove him off. I'm sure he'll be back any minute."

I narrowed my eyes at him trying to decide if he was lying or telling the truth. I decided to give Jake the benefit of the doubt. If anything bad happened to Quack, I would know, thanks to our special bond. Other than a growing bout of separation anxiety, I hadn't felt anything at all. Jake was safe from my wrath, at least for now.

"Wow." Jake took a step away from us and offered a cursory bow by way of goodbye. "Well, I won't keep you two. I appreciate the help. Sorry again. Maybe I'll see you around."

I raised an arm to tell him he was not about to go free when War lashed out with her broadsword and cut him in half.

Safe from my wrath, but apparently not hers.

I gasped in horror as Jake's hands went to his midsection. His face barely had time to register the surprise before he fell to the ground, in two bisected parts.

"What did you do that for?" I screamed at her.

"He's a Niner again. He'll emerge from the pools, and we'll have agents waiting for him."

"Yeah but ... we could have talked to him."

War shook her head and held out her hand. I looked at it then placed the locket in her palm. My mantle was gone and so were the other two. She was the only one left.

She, more than any of the rest of us underwent the biggest transformation. This time the sword not only clattered to the ground, but her armor melted away along with her helmet and mask revealing the blue hair and beautiful face hiding underneath.

"Alex?"

She took a deep breath and opened her eyes to look at me. "You didn't think I would let you fight this one alone, did you?"

"Well, yeah. I didn't think. How did you?"

"Come here." Alex laughed and pulled me into a kiss.

The questions racing through my mind slowed.

"It's over," Alex said as she backed away again with a smile. "You did it. You stopped the Four Horsemen. I can't believe you did it."

"Well, you helped."

"I did help." She tapped her finger on my chest. "And don't you forget it."

"I am so glad it's over." I let out a breath. "Although, there are going to be a lot of very confused people out there now that Simeon's not around to pull their strings anymore."

I had almost forgotten Simeon had gained control of his horde through modern technology. Now that he was gone, they should all be back to normal and the nanites infecting their brains should ... actually, I had no idea what they would do. It would take some sort of super genius to figure that part out.

As if on cue, Ryan groaned and stirred on the ground. "Simeon is not good. He is a bad man. He is not Ryan, I am Ryan." He stopped talking as if suddenly realizing he was able to form the words with his own mouth.

Recognition dawned in his face as he spun around to look and me and Alex. "Is he gone?"

The innocence in Ryan's eyes was so heartbreaking, I wanted to send Simeon into the coin all over again. Ryan, though brilliant, had severe autism among other things. How could anyone treat such an innocent soul the way Simeon had? Simeon deserved everything he got and more. I just hoped Ryan would be up to the task of undoing some of the bad Simeon did while he was here. Alex and I would have to make sure he stayed safe and give him the resources he needed. The world would see him as the great orchestrator of this nano-virus even though he had nothing to do with it. They would be looking for someone to blame, but Ryan needed to be their savior.

"Simeon is gone for good, buddy," I said. "He will never bother you again."

Ryan smiled and wrinkled his nose. "It smells bad in here. Why are you wearing a robe?"

Alex and I both laughed.

"Why are you still wearing that creepy costume? My armor melted away."

I looked down at myself and shrugged. "Modesty, I guess."

I waited for my meaning to register on Alex's face.

"You mean you're not wearing anything under ..."

I shook my head and grinned.

"Maybe you should keep that thing for a little longer. You and I can talk about what to do about it when we get back." She winked.

My eyebrows shot up so high they nearly flew off my head, but Alex turned her attention back to Ryan.

She walked over and took his hand, offering him a comforting smile. "Why don't we get out of here."

I made a makeshift bag out of Alex's coat and put all the artifacts inside, then we made our way out of the garage and headed up the street. People already seemed to be regaining some sense of themselves and although they were very confused, they seemed like they would be all right.

"I hate to say it, but this isn't quite over yet." I glanced over at Alex and then up the street again turning the artifact over in my pocket. "I know what the locket is now. Until we find a way to get rid of it, we will never be able to rest."

Alex's content smile turned down as she eyed me. "What is it?"

"Where do you guys think you're going without me?"

I smiled and looked up as Quack swooped in for a landing in front of us. I was happy to see his coloring back to normal and his feathers seemed to be in top-flight condition too.

"Ducky." Ryan exclaimed and reached out to pet him. I pulled him back and shook my head. "We shouldn't pet strange animals. We don't know where they've been."

Ryan nodded in understanding, eyeing Quack as he kept pace with us.

"Who are you calling strange. And thanks for your concern by the way. I could have been killed back there."

"If you had been hurt, I would have known it," I said. "Nice job by the way. You really came through for me."

Quack beamed with pride. "Still, you could have shown a little more concern. You have no idea how many bugs I had to swallow to stay airborne. I won't eat for a week."

"I never worried for a second, and I'll believe the eating thing when I see it." I chuckled.

"Don't listen to him," Alex said. "He was scared to death. And I'm glad you're safe."

"Thank you. At least somebody appreciates the efforts of a hero around here."

I rolled my eyes and kept walking. "Let's take care of Ryan, then get back to the agency and talk to Judas. I'll tell you about the locket on the way. He's going to want to hear about what happened to the Horsemen. Maybe it'll even soften the blow when we tell him about the true power of locket. If we're going to get out of his office in one piece, we are going to need all the good news we can get.

CHAPTER THIRTY-NINE

"And you disobeyed me yet again!"

Alex and I faced a very angry Judas Iscariot in his office. I had managed to change back into my regular clothes but was in no way comfortable. His face had worked its way into a deep shade of crimson and his voice vibrated the sheetrock. But he had not left his chair or sent Procel or Mastema over to pull our eyelashes off, so I took that as a good sign.

"I had the coin." I tried to interject.

Judas held up his hand to stop me. "Yes, your partner here told me all about the coin, but that does not preclude your intent to disobey my orders in the first place. You cannot fathom the repercussions had your little escapade gone badly."

"Escapade?" I said under my breath. "I think it was more of a stunt. A shenanigan at most."

Judas pounded his fist down on his desk making the three mantles we had laid on top jump into the air. "Millions died at your hand alone. Is there a joke you'd like to make about that?"

I shut my mouth and stared at the ground. He was right. There was nothing funny about all the deaths Topside, especially the ones I had a hand in.

"You know you're a bit of a hypocrite." Alex sat forward in her bone framed chair and eyed the furious looking Judas and he snapped his head in her direction.

"For all your talk about doing what has to be done for the better good, when Gabe stands up and does the same, all you want to do is chop his head off."

For the first time ever, Judas was left sitting with his mouth hanging open. He stared at her in stunned silence for a moment, then peered over at me.

"It seems I owe you an apology, Gabriel."

I pulled my gaze off the floor and looked from Judas to Alex and back again.

"Wait, you owe me what now?"

"An apology. Alexandrea is correct. You did what had to be done. Made a hard choice no matter the sacrifice and stood by your decision for the greater good. Had you not, all of humanity may have been lost. There are great tragedies to be mourned, but far less than there could have been. I commend you on your actions."

I wasn't all that sure about this complementary Judas. It made me feel warm and uncomfortable, like an old wool blanket that needed to be washed.

I let a small smile play across my face and nodded at him. "Thanks."

"For a guy who usually can't keep his mouth shut you're a man of few words all of a sudden." Quack sat on the floor between me and Alex. He was out of his backpack but promised not to move as Mastema might mistake him for the fuzzy rabbit in a greyhound race and turn him into a midday snack.

"How am I supposed to push his buttons when he is being nice?" I thought back. "Winning is way less fun than I thought it would be."

"As for Jake and Simeon," Judas continued. "We will have

agents waiting for them when they emerge from the pools. I'll arrange for a special ... reception for the both of them. No one will ever hear from those two again, I can assure you."

I held up my hand like a kid grade in school.

"Yes, Gabriel," Judas sighed. "You do not need to ask permission to speak."

Quack laughed in my mind. "That's better."

I put my hand down and smiled.

"Just a couple of side notes there. Don't be too hard on Jake. He did embrace the mantle, but he's not the sharpest set of scissors in the drawer. At the end, he regretted his decision and wanted out, but had no way to escape. If it weren't for him, we might have lost the battle altogether."

Judas nodded, considering my words but didn't say anything.

"And I don't think you'll have to worry about Simeon." I pulled the silver denarius out of my pocket and displayed it to him as if he could somehow see Simeon imbedded in the tarnished engraving. "He went right into the abyss of the coin. It must have been eager to get him back after his miraculous escape."

Judas looked down at the coin in my hand then at me again. "Are you sure?"

I thought about the horror and fear I saw on Simeon's face as he was sucked into the coin.

"I'm positive."

"What about Sammy?" Alex's expression was dark and full of menace. "She is the reason for all of this mess. Does she just get a free pass because she's an angel?"

Judas let out a laugh that made my skin want to crawl up my body and run away.

"Sammy got her wish. I have it on good authority that she was escorted uptown for a personal meeting with the judge.

There is no wrath in Hell like the Heavens' scorned. I can assure you she will beg for the mercy of the Gnashing Fields and will never receive it. Sammy will live out the rest of eternity atoning for her crimes, and no one will be there to hear her scream."

Judas's description ran a chill up my spine so cold I had to physically shake it off. Alex had lost her vengeful scowl, taking on an understanding, almost sorrowful expression instead.

"That leaves one last thing." I motioned to the three mantles laid out for display on Judas's desk. "We need to find a place to bury these things where no one will ever find them again."

Judas nodded. "It is more than a little problematic that all four are now located in The Nine."

"We think someone should bring two of them to heaven," Alex said.

Judas let out a little chuckle. "Unfortunately, I don't have a rogue angel on retainer. Transferring these will be more than a little complicated."

I held up a finger, interrupting him. "There is one other thing we need to tell you."

Judas took in a long breath then let it out again. I waited for him to complete his calming ritual. He would need it for this one.

I pulled the locket out from under my shirt and held it out for him to see. Judas appeared wholly underwhelmed.

"A necklace? Who does it belong to?"

"Funny thing." I laughed. "You have a way of always asking the right question."

Impatience crept into Judas's eyes, so I kept talking, determined to finish my explanation before he exploded again.

"This is an origin artifact." I held up my hand to cut Judas off as he opened his mouth to rage something at me. "I know, I should have told you about it sooner, but I had this in my possession way before you and I crossed paths. I knew it had power and always kept it hidden and safe. I just didn't know how much power."

I set the locket down on Judas's desk and went on.

"This artifact can bind or unbind items to the soul, or rather bind or unbind the soul to an item. It is an important distinction, because Simeon gave me the last piece of the puzzle right before the Denarius banished him to Never-Never Land. See, this isn't just an origin artifact. This is *the* origin artifact. You asked me who this belonged to. It belongs to Lucifer himself, much as he might wish it didn't. This is the original artifact used to bind his soul to the underworld, and he has been looking for it ever since. If he finds it, he can reverse the binding and return to Heaven."

For the second time in one day Judas was left dumbfounded.

"Alex and I discussed this a great deal. Someone needs to deliver two of these mantles to heaven and more importantly, this artifact should be delivered as well."

I picked up the locket and walked around Judas's desk to where he sat and placed it in his palm.

"You should be the one to go."

Judas just stared at me for a moment then peered down at the locket. I backed away and let it all sink in. Judas looked at us again and shook his head.

"Impossible. I need to run the agency. I can't possibly—"

Alex stood and cut him off.

"I have no doubt that Procel can find a suitable successor for your position. You held your post for long enough. It's time to go."

Judas stared at the two of us, holding the locket in his hand as if it were a precious drop of spring water he could not bear to spill.

"What if He doesn't want me?" His voice came out as nothing but a whisper and his naked profession brought a tear to my eye.

"He wants us all," I said. "The only reason we're here is

because of the choices we made in life. We made the wrong ones. It doesn't mean He loves us any less. You're the one person who is here because you made the right choice. You did what had to be done. You loved the Father so much you were willing to give everything to ensure the prophecy would be fulfilled. And you continued to make the hard choices for thousands of years." I swallowed the lump rising in my throat. "Now, it's time to let someone else take the reins. Go find your rightful place. Just don't forget about us down here in the basement."

Alex let out a sniffle and wiped at her eyes as I did the same. Judas let a single tear fall over his cheek and with it fell the weight of two thousand years. He let out a shuddering breath and nodded to me, then turned to Procel and muttered several words I could not understand. The huge albino demon nodded once showing no semblance of emotion before Judas turned to us again.

"All right." His face expressed fear, joy, tears, regret, hesitation and about a thousand other emotions. I was so used to seeing only anger that it almost didn't look like Judas at all.

"How does it work?"

"Holy crap, this is happening right now?" Quack said. "No party or anything? I figured there would be a cake or maybe a banner. Some sort of office going away thing."

"No time like the present." I thought back at him. "Just stay clear and let us figure this out before someone changes their mind."

"Will he have a forwarding address? This is all so sudden."

I ignored the rest of Quack's dialogue and wrapped Jake's pendant and the broadsword into a leather skin Judas had provided to store all the items in, leaving the top hat out.

"Take these." I placed the treasured package into his arms, retrieved the locket from his palm, then looped the sturdy chain around his neck allowing the locket to lay against his chest.

"Don't worry." Alex winked at Judas. "We know of a good place to hide the last mantle."

Judas walked out in front of his desk and stood there. "Is there some sort of incantation or ritual I need to perform?"

I shook my head. "You just kind of wish for it. Will it to life and the locket takes care of the rest."

Judas gave me a dubious look and I shrugged, not knowing what else to say.

Judas turned toward Procel and Mastema and bowed his head to each of them in turn. "Thank you for your service and loyalty over these centuries." Then he faced us again. "Please pass that message on to Terayn as well."

"We will." I smiled. "Now stop stalling. You've got this."

He nodded again, took a deep breath and closed his eyes then ...

"Wait!" Alex shouted, then ran over and threw her arms around his neck giving him a big hug. Then she leaned in and kissed him on the cheek. "Give that to my brother if you see him."

Judas had his arms full so he could not reciprocate and looked more than a little stunned at the kiss.

Alex stood back, clasped her hands at her chest and tried to blink away more tears.

"Okay, go ahead."

Judas stared at her, then at me. I just smiled and shot him a wink.

Judas closed his eyes again and the room went quiet. For several moments not a breath could be heard in the room.

Then Judas opened his eyes and shouted, "This is useless—" And in a flash of bright white light, he was gone.

We all stared at the spot where he had stood and then I let out a chuckle. "I sure hope the next word out of his mouth wasn't a cuss word."

I reached over and pulled Alex close to me, feeling like

something was altogether missing inside now. Judas was gone and although he usually yelled and screamed at me, he was my friend. He was a good man, and I would miss him.

I glanced at Mastema and Procel thinking they might be feeling the same. After all they had been together for thousands of years. The two demons, however, showed no emotion. I wasn't even sure they felt emotion.

"Well, we should be going I guess." I looked at the big albino demon. "If it's not too much to ask, would you mind putting in a good word with whoever takes Judas's position. I know it's against protocol, but Alex and I would really like to work together."

I let go of Alex and leaned down to open Quack's backpack so he could hop inside.

"I know how Denarii Division agents are supposed to work and all, but I think we could do some good as a team. Maybe work Topside on high profile cases and try to—"

"Done."

Procel's voice boomed off the walls in the room. The noise was so shocking I straightened before Quack made it all the way into the backpack, upending him beak first into the bottom. "Hey, watch it."

"Done?" I narrowed my eyes at Procel. "What do you mean done? Like you'll put in a good word or, done we can work together?"

"You will work together."

My eyebrows shot up in surprise and I glanced over at Alex. She looked just as shocked ... and slightly suspicious.

"Great," I said. "Thanks. Let me know when you find out who the successor is so we can stop by to—"

"Done."

This time I cringed.

"Now, wait a minute."

"Gabriel Gantry and Alex Neveu have been named as new

heads of the Judas Agency. Judas Iscariot has taken an extended leave of absence and will not be in contact within the foreseeable future. All operations and communications henceforth shall be directed to Gabriel Gantry and Alex Neveu the new heads of the Judas Agency.

"Stop talking like that." I waved my hands in the air trying to make him quit. "You sound like you're dictating a department memo."

"Correct. All agency members have been notified via department memo as of this moment."

"What?! How can you? I mean, you can just ..."

I looked over at Alex who seemed to be taking this much better than me.

"There are worse places for us to be, besides from here we can make sure nothing gets out of hand Topside."

"Are you serious? Us in charge of the Agency?" I shook my head. "This is crazy. Mastema, come on help me here. You know this is ridiculous. Tell them. I know you can talk."

She grinned and let out a cackle that sent shivers up my spine.

"Fine. Don't help me."

"Relax, Gabe." Alex walked around and sat gingerly in Judas's chair. "You'll need to bring in another desk of course."

"I ... what?" I ran my hands over my head and looked around the room.

"As your head cabinet advisor" Quack broke into my mind. "My first bit of guidance would be to calm down. No one is going to buy off on a prissy freak-out as the head of the Judas Agency. Freak out inside, look cool on the outside. That's how all the big dictators do it."

I took a breath and composed myself. "How would you know?"

Quack scoffed. "Stick with me. Everything will be all right."

I glanced over at Alex who appeared way too comfortable

behind Judas's desk. She grinned, no doubt hearing Quack's commentary as well.

I shook my head and smiled. Yeah, we would be all right, so long as we were together—as the new heads of The Judas Agency.

Did you love *Final Ruin?* Join the C.G. Harris Legion to stay up to date on upcoming books, receive book intel, useless trivia, special giveaways, plus you'll learn about Hula Harry and get his Drink of the Week. https://www.cgharris.net/legion-sign-up-page

Let other readers know what you thought of, *Final Ruin*, by Leaving a Review.

~

Haven't read the other books in The Judas File series? Get them now:

The Judas Files Completed Series:
    Book 1-THE NINE
    Book 2-NEW DOMINION
    Book 3-ARTFUL EVIL
    Book 4 - WAR ORIGIN
    Book 5 - FINAL RUIN

ABOUT THE AUTHOR

C.G. Harris is an award winning science-fiction and fantasy author from Colorado who draws inspiration from favorites, Jim Butcher, Richard Kadrey and Brandon Sanderson. For nearly a decade, Harris has escaped the humdrum of the real world by creating fictional characters and made-up realities. When not writing, Harris spends time collecting the illusive arcade token, from the golden age when Dig Dug and Frogger were king. Harris knows the value of such a collection will only be seen in the confused faces of those family members left behind long after C.G. Harris is gone.

Do you have questions, comments or ideas for future plots? Contact C.G. at: CGharrisAuthor@gmail.com